COIT
Chasing Chinatown Trilogy
Book Three

(Abby Kane FBI Thriller)

Ty Hutchinson

This book is a work of fiction. Names, characters, places, and incidents are the product of the author's imagination or are used fictitiously. Any resemblance to actual persons, living or dead, is coincidental.

All rights reserved. No part of this book may be reproduced, stored in a retrieval system, or transmitted in any form or by any means (electronic, mechanical, photocopying, recording, or otherwise) without the prior written permission of the author, Ty Hutchinson.

Published by Ty Hutchinson
Copyright © 2014 by Ty Hutchinson
Cover Design: Kay Hutchison

Suffolk Libraries			
Amaz			2/17

For my mother

COIT TOWER
Chasing Chinatown Trilogy
Book Three

(Abby Kane FBI Thriller)

Chapter 1

Team Balkan - Thessaloniki, Greece

The greasy ponytail may have hidden the hole in the back of his head, but the gushing sound of blood gave it away.

"It got in my eye!" shouted the man gripping the semi-automatic Zastava CZ99.

"What?" Drago Zoric looked over at his friend and saw him wiping at his face with the backs of his hands.

"His blood!" Branko Petrovic stopped momentarily and pointed the handgun at the man slumped over a weathered wooden table. "It splattered on my face," he said, hurrying over to the kitchen sink in the corner of the studio apartment. The faucet handle squeaked, and yellowish water sputtered into the shallow basin before turning mostly clear.

Zoric shook his head as he shoved an assault rifle into an old guitar case and locked the cover in place. "We have to get out of here." He bent down next to two other bodies that lay motionless on the floor and rummaged through their pockets before moving on to the one at the table.

When he finished, he made a quick survey of the decrepit apartment. The paint on the dull, white walls had bubbled and cracked. Stained linoleum curled up along the walls, revealing rotted floorboards beneath. Cobwebs draped the once-golden crown molding near the ceiling. It looked as if no one had lived there for years. Zoric let out a loud breath before walking over to the sheetless single bed against the wall and grabbing a silver briefcase off it.

"I'm sure some of that Greek pig's blood splashed into my eye," Petrovic ranted as he scooped water into his face.

"Let's go." Zoric walked toward the front door with the briefcase in one hand and the guitar case in the other. "There's not much time. I hear sirens. We must leave now."

Petrovic looked up. Water trickled down his face and collected in the three days' growth along his jawline. "That's what happens when you fire an AK-47 in a quiet neighborhood," he spat.

"Next time, don't stand so close when you pull the trigger," Zoric fired back.

"You left me no choice when you started shooting the other two."

"It's always the same with you: Blame me for everything."

"I thought we had a plan: tie them up and kill them quietly. Not with that cannon you lug around. Now the police are on their way."

"Right, so let's go."

Petrovic wiped his hands dry on his faded blue jeans before shoving his handgun into the waistband.

The two Serbians exited the apartment and quickly made their way down three flights of narrow stairs, the heels of their boots drumming the wooden steps along the way. They continued through a semi-lit hallway on the ground floor. A paisley carpet runner, tattered and barely holding its shape, led them to a door that opened into a small parking lot behind the building.

They walked briskly to a white delivery van they had stolen from a driver on his morning route. In the back of the vehicle, between shelves full of freshly baked bread, lay his body hidden under newspaper and flattened cardboard boxes.

Within seconds, they had pulled out of the lot and sped down the tight alley behind the building. The vehicle made a right onto the main drag that would connect them with the PATHE Motorway—a straight shot out of Greece and into Macedonia if all went well.

Zoric concentrated on the road ahead, breaking his gaze only to peek at the rearview mirror. No one seemed to be following them. Petrovic sat quietly in the passenger seat, fiddling with the lock on the security briefcase.

"You have to press both of the latches at the same time to open it," Zoric said, his eyes trained on the road.

Petrovic followed the instructions and a second later had the case open, revealing banded stacks of $100 USD. "We hit it big, Drago." He picked one up, but as quickly as his smile had formed, it disappeared. "What the fuck?"

"What?" Zoric grunted, still focused on the highway.

Petrovic picked up another banded stack and another, revealing that underneath lay stacks of cut newspaper. "We got ripped off." He flipped through the stack with the $100 bill. The first bill was real. The rest were scraps of newspaper. "Look at this shit," Petrovic said, holding up the worthless paper cuttings. "Those pigs planned to fuck us." He threw the briefcase into the back of the van.

"It's a good thing we fucked them first," Drago said.

"We're screwed. We just killed three of Stefanokos' soldiers."

"So?" Drago threw his shoulder up a bit.

"Kostas Stefanokos? The Godfather of Greece?" Petrovic shifted in his seat. "This was your idea. I should have never agreed to it." He dug into the front pocket of his leather jacket and removed a crumpled pack of cigarettes, plucking out a bent one. "'It'll be an easy score,' you said." The crooked smoke dangled between his lips, bobbing in sync with his words. "'We'll pretend to have a large shipment of cigarettes we need to unload,' you said," Petrovic continued, adding a wave of his hand.

"It was a good plan. We should be grateful it's not us lying in a pool of blood back there."

Petrovic shook his head as he exhaled loudly through his nose. "Look, these side jobs take our focus off our task." He struck a match and cupped his hand around it. His cheeks sunk as he took a long pull.

"We need the money."

"No, what we need to do is keep playing the game and win the prize."

Petrovic searched the other pocket of his jacket and removed his smartphone. He navigated to the Chasing Chinatown application and tapped the icon. A few seconds later, the app chimed. "We have a message."

Zoric glanced at Petrovic and then back at the road.

Petrovic had to reread it twice to be sure he understood it.

"What?" Zoric inquired.

"They changed the game."

"What are you talking about?"

"Now there is only one Attraction, and the first team to complete it wins ten million dollars."

Team Kitty Kat - Antwerp, Belgium

The slim woman wore a black latex one-piece and knee-high boots with chunky heels that escalated her stature to a towering six feet two inches. Her long red hair popped against her outfit, as did her slender ivory neck and hands. She stood in front of the floor mirror admiring herself while she applied more gloss to her already ruby-red lips before practicing her pout.

"Mistress," a timid voice called out, "I'm waiting to serve you."

Mistress Kitty was the persona that Adaira Kilduff had

adopted for her playdates. Through the mirror, she could see a man on his knees behind her, naked except for a silicone chastity belt.

Kilduff had agreed to meet with the man, a banker working in Belgium. He had spent the last half hour licking her boots, but she had grown bored and decided to spend time admiring herself. She did love the way she looked when in costume—the only type of dress-up the Scottish beauty preferred.

He was the first man she had decided to see while visiting Antwerp. He had gained access to an appointment by sending two thousand euros to her PayPal account. To be considered, she required a tribute to gauge the seriousness of all applicants who wanted a shot at being her pay pig.

Kilduff specialized in a very specific sort of play, one that very few men could afford to dabble in: financial dominatrix. The banker was in the process of auditioning to be her human ATM. She still hadn't given him an answer.

"I'm not sure you can afford to serve me."

"But I can. I will," he begged. "What do you want?"

The dominatrix spun around on her heels. "You know damn well what I want," she said in an elevated voice. "You do read, I presume. I made my wish list available before our meeting, and yet," she said, looking around the hotel room, "I see nothing from it."

"The Gucci purse." He motioned to the desk. "Don't you like it? I personally picked it—"

Crack! His head swung to the side from the force of her hand. Red welts in the shapes of her fingers rose on his cheek. "It's. Not. From. The. List."

Kilduff's patience had grown thin. She had neither the time nor the inclination to waste one more second with his disobedience. *His application seemed so promising,* she thought. Every now and then, even with her due diligence, she would end up with a pig who hadn't the means to meet her demands.

Kilduff differed from other financial dominatrices in that she *would* cross the line and threaten to out them to their wives, even make their fetish public, if their generosity faltered. She demanded tributes be in the form of cash or gifts from a specific wish list. But the biggest differentiating factor with Kilduff was how she dealt with the occasional problematic pig. She would eliminate them through strangulation disguised as autoerotic asphyxiation. Money drove her, and killing was just a means to an end.

Kilduff looked down at the whimpering man before her, debating whether to cut the session short. If she had been wrong about his financial situation, there really was no need to continue. She was irritated, of course, but not enough to dispatch him. She didn't kill out of anger. It was always for money.

"Please, let me try again. I promise to please you," he said, his voice barely a whisper.

"Fine. If you can pleasure me with your tongue, I'll

reconsider." Kilduff snapped her finger, and the pig followed her on his knees. She grabbed her cell phone off the mantel above the small fireplace before plopping herself down on a white leather sofa. She propped up one leg onto the cushion and left the other resting on the carpeted floor. This revealed the open slit in her latex suit. "Get to work."

Kilduff busied herself with her phone, uninspired thus far by the efforts of her pig. Sadly, her bank account was nearing depletion, and she had hoped this pig could provide the boost she needed to complete the game in Antwerp.

She watched as an animated Chinese dragon appeared on the screen of her phone. It snorted fire and danced around before morphing into the Chasing Chinatown logo. She thought about the inevitable, having to vet yet another potential, as the game finished loading. A few seconds later, she had a different thought.

<><><>

Team Lucky - Halfway between Melbourne and Sydney, Australia

Richie Pritcher brought the plastic-foil bag up to his chin and sent the remaining chips tumbling into his open mouth. He chewed and swallowed as he balled up the bag and aimed for a large plastic cup on top of a small table. He bricked his trash-ball off to the right against the window of the RV, sending it rolling off the table and under one of the pull-down sofas. *Next time.*

Pritcher couldn't be bothered with picking up the bag,

which crackled as it un-balled itself; he had rented the motorhome. Instead, he shrugged off his free-throwing abilities and wiped his hands on his T-shirt, completely oblivious to the orange smudges left behind.

Having successfully completed all of the Chasing Chinatown Attractions in Melbourne, Pritcher's next destination turned out to be Sydney. He thought a road trip would be a fun way to see the countryside. As his eyes searched the old RV, he scratched at the reddish-orange growth around his chin. His other hand dipped into his khaki cargo shorts and did the same with his flabby behind.

He stopped grooming himself only when he saw the wooden handle of the butcher knife he'd been looking for. It was partially hidden under a large bag of chocolate-covered raisins on the vehicle's kitchen counter.

Pritcher had one foot on the dry forest floor and the other still in the RV when he stopped. He looked back at the chocolate snack. He had already devoured half the bag earlier that morning and promised himself he would save the rest for later that night. He shifted his weight from foot to foot as his conscience did its best to fight his grumbling belly. A beat later, he grabbed the bag and exited the vehicle.

Completing the Attractions in Melbourne had been difficult for Pritcher. It had taken double the time he'd spent in Lima, Peru. Nothing seemed to go his way; he'd even had one of his submissions rejected for lack of creativity.

He had considered giving up in Melbourne, but the five-million-dollar prize was too much to pass up.

He'd rubbed his lucky rabbit's foot, purchased another horseshoe for the camper, refused to travel on Friday the thirteenth, avoided black cats, and continued to cross his fingers before every kill. Pritcher believed in those silly superstitions. He swore those were the reasons luck followed him in life. It was that belief that prevented him from actually quitting. *I'm the luckiest man alive*, he thought to himself. *Surely my lucky ways will prevail and make me rich.*

He tucked the knife under his left armpit, munched on a few raisins, and walked to the rear of the vehicle. There he rejoined the female hitchhiker he had picked up a few hours ago. She didn't serve a purpose for the game. She was merely for pleasure.

Earlier, he had tied her wrists to the rear bumper with an electrical cord and stuffed an old handkerchief into her mouth to keep her from screaming. He had spent twenty minutes talking to her and fondling her breasts through her shirt before nature called and forced him to the toilet in the RV.

Upon his return, her eyes widened, and he watched a tear escape from the corner of her left eye. She kicked her legs out in an effort to move away from him. She couldn't. Her white shorts were stained with the brown dirt that made up most of the surrounding terrain.

Pritcher smiled at the woman and asked in a friendly tone, "Would you like some raisins?"

She responded with a muffled cry.

Before he could say anything else, the front of his shorts buzzed. "Excuse me." He placed the knife and the bag of treats on the bumper and removed his cell phone from his pocket. He had a message from the game. *Good news, I hope.*

He almost choked on the last handful of raisins he had popped into his mouth. *No way!* He spun around in delight as laughter and a few chewed raisins spewed forth from his mouth. "I can't believe it. Ten million dollars."

Pritcher read the message again and again while walking absentmindedly in a circle. When he turned back to the girl to share the news, six inches of stainless steel were driven into his chest.

He pulled in a sharp breath as he stared at the handle of the knife. He felt no pain, only pressure where it had been driven into him. *How?* His eyes darted to the bumper; the electric cord lay in the dirt below it.

The woman stood in front of him. Her tears had cut through the dirt on her face, leaving prominent streaks. Her breathing erratic, her eyes fastened on the knife. She let go of the wooden handle and backed away slowly, eventually turning and running from him as fast as she could. Her bare feet kicked up puffs of dirt behind her as she disappeared into a patch of trees.

Pritcher, still confused by what had just happened, lowered himself to the ground and leaned against the RV's bumper. The front of his shirt grew heavy and warm. With each breath, the knife moved up and down. Slowly he placed his hand around the handle, careful not to disturb it. He then held his breath, counted to three, and yanked.

Chapter 2

That day, the temperature in San Francisco was unseasonably high—eighty degrees Fahrenheit. Special Agent Scott Reilly had both of his hands resting on his waist. He had removed his suit jacket earlier and loosened his tie. He stared at the cloudless sky, lost in thought. I kept an eye on the two agents from the bureau as they performed a perimeter walk around my property. Only when they disappeared along the side of my home, heading toward the backyard, did I interrupt my supervisor's daydream.

"Is this really necessary?" I asked.

"Huh?" It took a few seconds for my question to break through the cloud in his head. "Abby, look, we have to take precautions. It's a credible threat. I can't let it go."

A week ago, Reilly and I had found out that the mastermind behind the Chasing Chinatown game had placed a bounty on my head worth ten million dollars. Every sicko playing the game had been given a final task—winner-take-all—with a sizeable jackpot providing the incentive to travel to San Francisco and deliver my noggin.

"I realize that, but do you really think you need to embed two agents in my *home*?"

"Don't fight it. Until we can better assess what we're up against, this is how it'll be. You're lucky I'm not placing an agent on you. By the way, where are we on an active team count?"

"In the last week or so, the dragonheads of five Chinatowns were arrested. All have been confirmed to be managing the game in their respective city. That leaves nine cities, but word about the new Attraction had already been made when they were shut down. So technically, any team with access to the game app probably got the message. I'm guessing somewhere between nine and fourteen."

Reilly ran a hand over his face. "Christ, that's exactly what I'm talking about. We don't know how many teams are active and will come after you. Team Carlson and Team Creeper are the only ones confirmed to be inactive, and that's because they're dead."

I couldn't argue with Reilly. Our entire strategy of shutting the game down had moved away from catching the players to disrupting the gameplay itself by removing the ones responsible for managing it.

I spied my mother-in-law, Po Po, peering at us from the dining room window. Even though I had only been married to her son Peng for a short time, his death actually made me feel closer to her, maybe because a part of him existed within her. I had always considered her family, even if she didn't approve of me. She shook her head and disappeared behind the curtain.

After Reilly had informed me of his plans that morning, I called Po Po to let her know we would be having guests. Her reply: a loud breath followed by a remark about readying the guest room and fixing extra food for dinner. As though she ever underprepared for meals.

I turned my attention back to Reilly. "How about one agent?" I said, not wanting to turn my home into Fort Knox just yet.

He shook his head. "This is how it'll work. Two agents will remain on the premises at all times. They will also be responsible for escorting the kids to and from school and play dates, as well as accompanying your mother-in-law, should she need to run an errand or whatever she does." Reilly took a step forward. "Let's catch up with them." He motioned with his head.

We followed the same narrow and grassy path alongside the old Victorian. Reilly pocketed his hands as we walked. "Did you say you installed motion-sensor lighting in the backyard?"

I nodded. "After the call from the Monster, but the neighbors complained. I get a lot of rogue raccoons on my property, so it's temporarily disabled for now."

The Monster was the nickname given to a fugitive on the FBI's list of most wanted criminals. He had contacted me a few months ago, claiming to be standing in my backyard. He had lied, but it was enough of a wake-up call that I had the floodlights installed. Up until that point, all we had had was a meek 45-watt bulb over the backdoor of the enclosed patio.

"Time to annoy the neighbors again," he said.

The yard was thirty feet wide, twenty feet long, and surrounded by a ten-foot-tall hedge thick enough to provide privacy, but there were areas where a small person could pass through if they wanted. I know so because I did it once.

Off center stood a seventy-five-foot Ponderosa pine. The base had a span of seven to eight feet. While the branch coverage for this particular variety of pine wasn't especially thick, it still added to the dark cover at night.

One of the agents, Marty Castro, approached us. He was a stocky fellow who wore a thick mustache. Most agents were clean cut, but Castro relished his lip fur. "The hedge creates a natural buffer, but I recommend we secure it with additional fencing, green plastic that can blend—"

"No fences. The property is relatively secure," I said.

Castro was our in-house expert on setting up safe houses. He could assess a property for weaknesses and determine how much of a viable threat existed in less than ten minutes. Scary accurate would be the best way to describe his abilities. With that said, I still wanted to minimize the intrusion so as not to freak the family out any more than needed.

"You have to think like them, Abby," he told me. "Think like a person who's got nothing to lose and is willing to get to someone no matter what."

I had to wonder how badly those teams playing the game wanted to get to me. Is ten million dollars enough motivation to come after an FBI agent? Does a serial killer have something to lose? Yes, his anonymity.

Castro pointed at the floodlights attached to both corners of the roof. "Are those motion sensitive?"

"Yes, but they're disabled right now because of the neighbors. That's their bedroom right there." I pointed at a window just above the hedge. "I thought of downgrading them to a lower wattage and reinstalling them to the patio roof."

Castro looked over his shoulder at the neighbor's house. "Lowering them would solve that problem. Definitely a good idea to get them operational again."

Reilly cleared his throat. "All right, Marty, this is officially your detail. Abby, you're in good hands." He gave me a nod before turning on his heels and walking back toward the front of the house.

Castro and I watched him until he disappeared.

"It's all business with him, isn't it?" Castro remarked.

I shrugged. "It's the shell he wears. Underneath, he cares."

The agent who accompanied Castro appeared from the other side of the house.

"Anything?" Castro called out.

The agent shook his head. "No blind spots up front."

Castro waited until the agent closed the distance before

making an official introduction. "Abby, this is Agent Kip Lin. He's new to the team, but he's good. You've got nothing to worry about."

I shook Lin's extended hand. "I'm not worried." I hadn't seen him around the office, but it's always nice to meet a fellow agent who's Chinese.

"So what's the plan? What happens next?"

Castro looked at his watch. "School should be finishing soon, right?"

I nodded.

"I'll have Agent Lin escort your children back to the property. At that point, I'll go over a few rules for the family. Don't worry; I'll keep it informal. I know this is an intrusion, but it's for the best. The most important thing is that your mother-in-law and children understand that they're not allowed to go anywhere without an escort. Other than that, your family should carry on with their daily routines. Agent Lin and I will stay as inconspicuous as possible."

"Tell you what: I'll pick up my kids. When we get back, you can officially take over." Picking up the kids would give me an opportunity to prep them about the situation. Plus, I could imagine Lucy running away from Lin since I had drilled it into her head that she shouldn't talk to strange men, even if they claimed they knew me.

Castro smiled. "We have prep work we can attend to. We'll see you when you get back."

That night, I insisted that Castro and Lin eat with us at the dinner table. I thought the more informal their presence, the better. Po Po, not surprisingly, had whipped up a feast. While I fetched the kids, Lin drove her to Chinatown, where she picked up two whole roasted ducks, stocked up on fresh vegetables, bought a couple of slabs of pork ribs to roast, and picked out a large carp that she had steamed for us in a ginger soy sauce. I had a feeling she wouldn't have any problems adjusting.

"This is a wonderful meal, but I'm afraid I won't be able to do my job if I'm stuffed like a turkey," Castro said, forking another serving into his mouth.

A sliver of a smile appeared across my mother-in-law's face. I knew she liked the attention. "You must eat. Keep up your strength." She balled up a fist and shook it before shuffling back into the kitchen. *I swear those house slippers are grafted to her feet.*

Castro sat to my right. "Don't fight it," I whispered, leaning toward him. "Just enjoy it."

The kids took our situation in stride. Ryan peppered both agents with questions all throughout dinner, wanting to know what kind of work they did, what cases they worked on, if they had ever disarmed a bomb. I don't know where that last question came from. He had never asked me that.

Lucy remained quiet at first but eventually overcame her shyness when Lin made a quarter appear from her ear. After I tucked both kids into bed and said good night to Po

Po, I joined Castro in the enclosed patio. "Where's your partner?"

"He's positioned on the front porch. He's got first night's duty. He'll remain there but make scheduled rounds around the perimeter. I'll relieve him at five a.m."

"I wondered how the sleeping arrangements would work, seeing that the guest room only has one bed."

Castro chuckled. "We'll never sleep at the same time. Push comes to shove, I can always bed down right out here. I like the outdoors." He turned his gaze back to the blackness of the yard and resumed tugging on his mustache.

The night air was cool and fragrant with pine. It was relatively quiet save for the pulsating chop of a news copter that passed overhead. I sat in the patio chair next to Castro and sipped my favorite green tea from a large mug.

I had almost forgotten about Castro until he cleared his throat.

"How credible is the threat?"

I didn't bother to look at him when I answered. "They'll come."

Chapter 3

The following morning, I rose earlier than usual for a Saturday, around six. The kids wouldn't wake for another hour, and Po Po was still sound asleep from what I could hear—no noise coming from the kitchen. I checked in on Castro, who had by then taken up the post on the front porch. We made small talk for five minutes about nothing in particular before I left and headed to my office on the third floor. I wanted to familiarize myself with the remaining teams and try to determine who might actually be in a position to take on the mastermind's offer.

In the nook I called my office, I sipped green tea that had just finished steeping, and I stared out the tiny window that overlooked the front yard while I waited for the Chasing Chinatown game to boot up on my laptop. Initially I thought to focus on the teams whose physical distance was near San Francisco. They seemed most likely to take the mastermind up on his offer. Then again, we were dealing with deranged individuals, and what seemed likely wouldn't necessarily equate with their actions.

I navigated to the map of the world and the leaderboard. Technically, there were still fourteen teams in play, and none of them were in the States. But with every dragonhead we arrested, that meant one less Chinatown to host the game. According to the map, the nearest team was in Mexico City. But I knew I couldn't base everything on distance. Any one of the teams was only a flight away. Since every team went by a nickname and used an avatar, I had no idea who these people were or what they even looked like. Problematic? Yes. My enemy was invisible.

When a team completed an Attraction, that was how I tracked them. A pop-up message would appear informing everyone of a team's success. If a team had been successful in completing all the Attractions in a city, I would receive an alert, but after that, they essentially went dark until they completed an Attraction in a new city. Being that I was the sole Attraction, I couldn't tell who had decided to come after me. The game, previously an asset to my investigation, had begun to showcase its limitations.

Even though we had no concrete evidence suggesting the teams would actually pursue an FBI agent, we had to act as though they were stupid enough to do so. Reilly and I talked at length about that possibility, and we both came to the conclusion that it was real. Coming after me wasn't a smart move, but playing the game wasn't either.

Given the sophistication of the game and what we'd encountered so far, we knew we weren't dealing with garden-variety killers. They were experienced and smart enough not to get caught playing a game that dictated where and when they killed. I had to give the teams credit for that. Most of our success thus far had come from eliminating the game's management, not the players themselves.

What I had learned about serial killers over the years told me they most likely wouldn't come after me. It would pose too much of a risk for them, despite the possibility of a ten-million-dollar payout. But I couldn't be sure; a nagging feeling had me doubting my initial assessment. There was absolutely no way to determine if each team fit the psychological profile of a serial killer simply by following their actions through the game. I had to rely on my gut and my experience in dealing with these types. I imagine there was a good chance some of the teams were opportunistic—outright thugs looking for a quick and easy payday.

Before I could give my predicament any more thought, a drawn-out yawn caught my attention. I spun the leather chair around to find Lucy standing in the doorway. She still had her Hello Kitty pajamas on, and a stuffed panda bear was tucked under her arm.

I held my arms out, inviting her to climb up on my lap, which she promptly did. "Why are you up so early? You have another half hour of sleep at least."

"I'm not tired," she said, rubbing her left eye on Wonton's head. That was what she had named her panda bear. "What are you doing?"

"Mommy's working."

"You catching bad men?" Her eyes opened wider.

"Yes, I'm catching them."

A smile stretched across her face. "Good."

I gave my munchkin a squeeze and a few noisy pecks to the top of her head. She was getting taller and heavier, but I would never stop her from sitting on my lap. She could be thirty, married, and have kids, and I would eagerly motion her to sit.

"Mommy?"

"Yes?"

"How long are your friends staying with us?"

"I'm not sure, honey. They are here to help me."

"Are they part of our family now?"

I thought about what Lucy had said for a moment. Castro and Lin were living with us rent free and helping themselves to whatever we had in the fridge. If that wasn't family, what was? "Yes, sweetie. They are part of our family."

Lucy giggled. "The short one is always playing with his moochas."

"It's mustache."

"Moochas."

"Mus-tash."

"Moo-chas."

Close enough. "Come, why don't you go brush your teeth before your brother gets up? You know how long he takes in the bathroom."

"Forever. Like a girl."

"Your brother's not a girl. He's just very detailed with his grooming." Lucy wasn't exaggerating. Ryan had, over time, developed a routine in the morning that could last as long as thirty minutes, which if you ask me, was strange for a nine-year-old boy going on ten.

"I have to get the spikes just right," he had told me.

Lucy slid off my thigh and exited my office, dragging Wonton behind her. I spun around just as my cellphone vibrated on the wooden desk.

"Abby, it's Kyle. Am I calling too early?"

"No, it's fine. What's up?"

"The street fair. Today is the open house of the Hop Sing Tong. I know you got the security detail, so I'm checking to see if you're still game to go."

"Of course I am. The detail is for the kids and my mother-in-law. I talked Reilly out of giving me a shadow. Though I'm not sure if I should bring the family."

"Bring them. It'll be fun. The agents can watch over them as we case the tong. Plus there's somebody I want to introduce you to."

It was set. Kang and I made plans to meet at the south entrance to Waverly Place, just off of Sacramento, around eleven thirty. That would give Castro plenty of time to think about our little outing and how he wanted to handle it.

Chapter 4

I had to admit, the street fair that the Hop Sing Tong had organized took me by surprise. I expected a table outside the tong with a couple of members greeting people, maybe a food booth or two, and something fun for kids, like a face painter.

Instead, the tong had the entire street shut off from vehicle traffic. Food and merchant booths ran the entire length. There were face painters and clowns making balloon animals, a variety of carnival games, even a pony ride. The tong had gone all out in an effort to present a different, positive face to the community. What had once been a stronghold for Triad gang activity now masqueraded as a recreational center for the residents of Chinatown. At least, that was how it came across to me. And that was exactly what they wanted.

As I looked at the sea of people in front of me munching on Chinese finger food, playing pin the tail on the dragon, and shopping for sandalwood and teak carvings, I wondered if I were alone in that thinking. Did the people at the fair really believe the tong had changed its ways, or were they simply enjoying the moment and not giving it much thought?

Kang and I broke off from the family almost instantly after arriving. Castro and Lin set off with the kids and Po Po while Kang and I talked more about my situation.

"You know what I don't understand?" Kang said as he steered me to a booth selling egg rolls. "Why target you and not me? I'm as much a part of this investigation as you are."

"If you want, I can message the mastermind and see if he'll include you so you don't feel left out."

Kang motioned to the vendor with two fingers, and within seconds, two large egg rolls fresh out of a vat of hot oil were dumped into a couple of paper trays. Kang grabbed a handful of towels and handed half of them to me along with an egg roll. "That's all right. I'm not that eager to become a target. It just doesn't make sense for them to single you out. Anything come to mind on why that would be?"

I took a moment to think about his question. I also took that moment to take a tiny bite of my egg roll. The crispy outer shell crackled as my teeth sank into the golden-brown cylinder. Enough of the insides spilled onto my tongue for me to realize the roll would rock once it cooled down. Kang blew on his eggroll twice before biting it in half.

"Nothing jumps out," I said before I sucked a whistle of air into my mouth to cool off the bite I had just taken. "I keep trying to think about moments or interactions I might have had without you. Two come to mind: the meeting I had with Somchai, the guy who managed the game in Bangkok."

"Yeah, yeah, I know who you're talking about. Let me guess the other—the girl you interrogated, the assassin. What was her name?"

"Sei. Well, that's the name she gave us."

Kang puckered his lips for a few seconds. "Maybe something you said or did during that interrogation made you a threat, because if you remember correctly, I did meet that girl on two separate occasions." Kang popped the last of his roll into his mouth and brushed his hands together.

Mine had cooled enough for me to seriously attack it. "You said earlier you had someone you wanted to introduce me to."

"Yeah, but I don't see her yet. Let's head over to the tong. She might be there."

Kang led the way, snaking a trail through the crowd as his height cast a shadow over my petite frame. "By the way, where's your girlfriend?" I asked between bites.

"She's at the station working on some big story."

Suzi Zhang, or Dragon Woman, as I liked to call her, was an anchorwoman for KTVU TV station located across the Bay in Oakland. She'd had a rocky relationship with Kang a few years ago before taking a job in Florida. Now back in town, she'd since reconnected with him. Clearly he hadn't learned his lesson the first time around. "Is the story about fresh-pressed juicing and how some juicers fresh press very little of their supply? No, wait. I know. Oil pulling: Is it really the cure all we think it is?" I mimicked a marquee with my hands for added effect.

Kang shook his head. "Why can't you two get along?"

"Annoying comes to mind," I mumbled.

"What?"

"I said these egg rolls were a good find."

"I heard you."

Then why did you ask? In an effort to quickly change the subject, I pointed at a building about twenty feet away. "There's the tong."

"And there she is," Kang said.

Only one woman was noticeable among the crowd standing outside the tong. Not because she had dressed her short and stout frame in white slacks with a bright red and yellow top or pulled it all together with an equally colorful wooden necklace with large beads leading to an enormous flower pendant. It also wasn't her long red nails or the multitude of jade bangles that encircled each arm. What did it for me was the fat cigar she had clasped between her fingers, the one that she waved in front of her as she addressed a group of individuals that had formed a half circle around her. They all leaned in with their heads slightly turned. The cigar didn't seem to faze them, but I had zeroed in on it and couldn't take my eyes off of it. It's not often that one sees a fifty-something Chinese woman puffing on a cigar out in public.

We were too far to hear any of the conversation, but something she said caused the group, including her, to erupt into bowed-over, loss-of-breath laughter. By the time we were within earshot of the group, the show was over, and they were dissipating.

"Ethel," Kang called out.

The woman, now fully composed, spun around, and her eyes settled on my partner. She smiled, causing her cheeks to bulge. "Kyle, you made it."

"I see you still have the habit," he said.

She held up her hand, giving me a better look at the smoking brown stump. "What, this? I only smoke them on special occasions." She looked around, eyes wide. "I believe this is one of them."

Kang bent down and gave the woman a hug. After pulling away, he said, "I'd like you to meet a friend of mine. This is Abby Kane."

The woman flashed me the same smile and extended her right hand. "Ethel Wu. Pleasure to meet you."

"Same here."

"Abby is an agent with the FBI," Kang pointed out.

"FBI? Chinatown has you to thank for clearing out the undesirables from the Hop Sing Tong."

"A lot of individuals were involved, including Kyle. By the way, how did you two meet?" I asked.

"I've known this man for at least fifteen years," she said, glancing at Kang for confirmation.

He nodded. "Yeah, I'd say that sounds about right. Ethel and I first met when I was just a beat cop making the rounds in Chinatown. One day while on a lunch break, I stopped by the CCBA over on Stockton—"

A crinkle must have formed on my brow.

"It's short for Chinese Consolidated Benevolent Association," he quickly followed up.

"I'm not familiar with the organization."

"They look out for the rights of Chinese Americans, specifically immigrants. There are branches in almost every major city of the U.S."

"Kyle wanted to know more about the history of our association," Ethel continued. "I thought it strange at the time. Students needing information for a school project are the ones stopping by, but a young police officer?" she said with a playful eye roll. "That was a first."

She took a couple of short pulls on her cigar. White, billowing smoke shot out from her mouth as the end burned brightly back to life.

"Ethel was the one who encouraged me to take my interest in Chinese history seriously."

"He had a knack for it. It would have been a shame if he hadn't," she added.

"Do you still work at the CCBA?" I asked.

Kang answered. "Ethel ran the CCBA when I first met her and still does to this day."

"What can I say? I'm passionate about what we do."

32 *Coit Tower*

"I'm guessing your presence here means the association supports the reopening of the tong."

"It does. We believe second chances are needed in life. The tong has made it very clear that they are committed to community improvement."

I couldn't tell whether her words were genuine or if it simply was political speak, but I decided not to question it further.

"You have to tour the tong. The first two floors are open to the public."

What about the other three floors?

Ethel walked us over to a portable table where four women sat. "The tong is asking that all visitors sign in before entering. One of these lovely volunteers from the CCBA will serve as your guide and can answer any questions you might have."

"Thanks, Ethel." Kang gently squeezed her arm before she departed.

After Kang and I signed in, one of the women sitting behind the table stood and came around to the front. "Hello, I'm Mable Chun. I'll be your guide."

The first floor of the tong housed a reception area and a small informational library with ample seating for visitors. The second floor housed a conference room, a kitchen, a couple of offices, and a recreation room where, I guessed, members could congregate and play mahjong or whatever it was they did here. The walls were decorated with Chinese art, and a few pieces of antique teak furniture dotted both floors. The place was straightforward. Nothing I saw appeared helpful toward our investigation.

"Do you have any questions?" our guide asked.

"What's on the other floors?" I pointed at a staircase that had been roped off.

Mable was an elderly Chinese woman who wasn't much taller than me. She had embraced the gray and kept it short with curls. Brown age spots covered her arms, but she had pep in her walk. I had to assume she was in her seventies, around Po Po's age. With a sweet smile, she said, "You know, they don't tell us what's up there except that it's used for storage." A crinkle appeared on her brow. "If you ask me, seems like a terrible waste of space." I couldn't agree more. *What could they possibly be storing that required three entire floors?*

Chapter 5

Our short tour of the tong had us back outside and dodging sidewalk traffic fairly quickly. A man walked by us with a plate held up to his face, slurping a large, white noodle into his mouth. That could only mean one thing.

"Someone is selling chow fun," I said, punching Kang in the arm. "Let's find that booth."

My head swiveled back and forth as I pushed through the crowd. The egg roll I had eaten earlier hadn't done much to quell the rumbling in my stomach. In fact, it had only intensified the growl.

"Not much came out of the tong tour," Kang said, catching up.

"We're exploring angles."

"You have a bounty on your head, and our only person of interest is an assassin who has all but disappeared off the face of this earth. Time isn't what we have. We need to figure out a way to eliminate that prize offer. No money, no reason to come after you."

"You'd think," I said.

"It's a start."

"Let's not rule out the tong just yet. I feel like there's a connection that we're not seeing. It wasn't long ago that the place was teeming with Triads charged with managing the game. I don't buy that a street fair changes all of that."

"We might find an answer on one of those top three floors. I'll get the ball rolling on a search warrant."

"Great."

"What about our mysterious assassin? Have you picked up any more information, aside from what you've already gathered?"

Kang was referring to the information my protégée, Leslie Choi, had turned over. She had assumed my old position as head of the OCTB, the Organized Crime and Triad Bureau, in Hong Kong. The intel came from a contact she had with the Shanghai police force. "Nothing really. They think she's a gun-for-hire who works for underground organizations like the Triads. She's not a person of interest as far as they're concerned. But Reilly mentioned he would reach out to a contact with the CIA who had spent time in Asia."

Kang bobbed his head from side to side. "Every lead needs to be chased down."

"I'll email you what I have. Maybe you'll see something I haven't."

We found the food booth serving up chow fun and stood in line.

"You know what still bothers me?" Kang asked as he studied the menu of offerings.

"What?"

"The Triad involvement. I still don't get why. Even if they were making money on some sort of entry fee for playing the game, how much could they realistically charge these killers for something they could do for free?"

"It's not a solid enough reason to be involved. And I don't think the game is something they developed. Whoever is behind it recruited the gang. There's a connection that we're not seeing, and getting to Sei might give us an answer."

When we reached the front of the line, a smiling teenage girl took our order. We both opted for the beef chow fun. In the makeshift kitchen behind her was a thin man dressed in a white undershirt and a stained apron. He stood over an industrial-sized steel wok that had blue and yellow flames licking the bottom.

Wielding a metal spatula and ladle, he made quick work of the sliced flank steak he had just dropped into the rounded frying pan. As he tossed the beef to a golden brown, the clanking and scraping of the utensils played a tune that was music to my ears.

He dipped the spatula into containers housing chopped garlic, black pepper, and hoi sin sauce. Into the steak mixture the ingredients went, fueling the sizzle of the searing oil one by one.

Flip. Flip. Flip. Green onions. Flip. Flip. Flip. Sliced onions.

After a few more tosses and turns, in went the noodles, dampening the lovely hiss but upping the aroma. And just as quickly as he had gathered the ingredients into the wok, he scooped them out, dividing them up between two paper plates.

Kang and I spent the next ten minutes slurping, chewing, and swallowing chow fun that was much too hot to be slurped, chewed, and swallowed that quickly. But when it came to food, we were dumb like that.

When our plates were empty, we caught up with the kids and Po Po to enjoy the rest of the day the best we could, which was a little hard because, you know, I had a bounty on my head.

Chapter 6

We made it though the rest of the weekend without any incident. Castro and Lin had settled into our home with minimal intrusion, and I didn't foresee any problems arising from their presence. It seemed as though each member of the family had accepted them for their own reasons.

For Lucy, they were two other people she could play with. Ryan took advantage of every opportunity to pick their brains. Po Po loved that applause for her culinary skills came from someone other than us. And I, well, so long as everyone had a smile, I was happy.

That Monday morning, I woke earlier than usual and relaxed with a cup of green tea. Usually it's a mad rush to get the kids and myself ready for the day. I'm almost always left with waiting until I get to work to have my first sip, unless I have time to fill a travel mug for the commute, which is almost never.

I fixed Castro a cup of coffee and chatted with him for a bit on the front porch. He sat on the wooden railing, one leg touching the ground, the other left dangling. I plopped my butt down in a rattan papasan chair, pulling both feet up and tucking them under me.

He wanted to know how I would proceed with my investigation, given the fact that I had become a target.

"It's business as usual." I took my first sip and swallowed, chasing the warmth down my throat. "I'm running down leads and hoping they point me to the mastermind."

"What's your best assessment on his location?" Castro took two large gulps, nearly finishing his coffee.

"More?" I motioned to the cup in his hand.

He shook his head and balanced the mug on the railing.

"Hard to tell." The truth: I had no idea. Initially I'd thought the mastermind was in the States, but my trip to Bangkok made me think otherwise. I'd had a feeling he was there, watching me. "I think he's mobile, able to move from city to city with ease. I don't believe he's a fugitive or even a POI for any law enforcement agency."

Castro raised both eyebrows, forming thick rows along his forehead. "That makes it harder. He's hiding in the open. What's your lead?"

Up until that point, I had withheld details from Castro, mostly because he wasn't actively working the case, but I realized throughout this investigation, I had gotten no closer to identifying the mastermind. I needed the help.

"I'm sorry. I'm prying. It's not my case."

I must have been mulling longer than I thought. "You're fine. I could use a sounding board."

Castro smiled, giving his thick mustache a bit of

thinness. "We're all on the same team. What do you have so far?"

I brought him up to speed on the gameplay and how the Triads managed it locally. "That's the Chinatown connection. We put two and two together when we gained access to the game and were able to masquerade as Team Carlson."

Castro said nothing as I summarized my trip to Bangkok and my altercation with Sei.

"So a tong that's turned over a new leaf and a female assassin that has a better disappearing act than a Vegas magician. You have two long roads to follow."

"Any thoughts?" I asked.

Castro tugged at his mustache as his eyes darted to the wooden floorboards of the porch. The baby-blue paint was weathered and cracked. "Well, until you hit the tong with a search warrant, it's still a viable angle. Could be something there. I'd do the same. But the girl, that's the wildcard. But from what you've told me, she's your best bet, if you can locate her."

"And that's the problem. Aside from catching one of these killers alive and questioning them, I'm really hoping a search of the tong turns up something useful. The connection between the Triads and the game never made much sense to me. It's not characteristic for them to be involved with it."

"Maybe they're not the ones behind it."

"They're managing the game on a local level."

"I'm not denying that, but maybe they're being paid to do it. Maybe their involvement is purely contractual. A job for them."

I nodded. "It certainly makes more sense: another form of income." I glanced at my watch. It was time to get the kids in motion and myself ready for work.

"Don't beat yourself up, Abby."

"What makes you think I am?" I asked, raising an eyebrow.

"Because if I were you, I might be inclined to do the same. You think your two leads are crap, right?"

Castro was right. My conversation with him had reminded me of that fact.

He slid off the railing and shook his left pant leg straight. "There is one thing you should take solace in. The bounty on your head... it's a deterrent. It's meant to slow you down. At one point, you were close, whether you realize it or not."

What Castro said made a lot of sense. The more I occupied myself with staying alive, the less focused I would be on finding the mastermind. Something I said, did, or saw was enough to spook the mastermind—enough for him to come after me. Either that or I was a mosquito that he had grown tired of swatting away.

I thanked him for his input and headed back inside knowing full well that my case was on track. I just didn't know how.

Chapter 7

I waved goodbye to the kids even though I couldn't see them through the blacked-out windows of the agency-issued SUV. Lin had the responsibility of chauffeuring the kids to and from school. Once they were out of my eyesight, I got into the driver's seat of my new car—a black Dodge Charger, complete with 370-hp HEMI V8. It gave me balls.

I know what you're thinking: *Gee, Abby, aren't you a little too small for that car?* Shut up.

Up until a few months ago, I'd had an Impala. While it provided plenty of room for the family, it was boxy and didn't have the handling I needed. I had no choice but to kick it to the curb and get a four-door that wasn't afraid to corner and tackle hills.

I had just backed out of my driveway when Kang rang me on my cell. "Abby, I just picked up the search warrant for the tong. Let's hit it ASAP."

"I'll meet you outside the tong in fifteen minutes."

"See you soon."

I threw the black beast into gear but didn't punch the gas. I figured Kang had either paid an early-morning visit to a judge's home or met them at the courts—most likely the second of the two—so he would be coming from the Civic Center, and I would easily beat him to the location.

Exactly fifteen minutes later, I turned onto Waverly Place. I parked fifty feet away from the entrance of the tong and waited in my car. Foot traffic was minimal, and besides mine, there were only a few other cars parked on the street. Most of the small shops hadn't opened yet. The restaurant on the corner of Waverly and Clay had, though.

From my vehicle, I had an unobstructed view of the tong's building. Nothing about it stood out; it looked much like the other tongs located on the lane. It stood five stories tall and had been constructed mostly with red brick. A platform fire escape snaked its way down the front of the building. Plastered across the railings were forest green billboards with gold lettering touting the tong's name. A double glass door with a dark limousine tint sealed the front entrance.

While I waited for Kang, I checked my email from my phone. I saw one from Reilly. He wanted to see me as soon as I got to the office. I emailed him back that I would follow up with him as soon as Kang and I were done searching the tong.

I thought a little about what Castro had said to me earlier that morning, about the bounty on my head being a deterrent, and wondered if it really was just that. Maybe we were the only team that got the message, and it was a way to send us off into a never-ending chase of our tails and allow the game to continue without interference.

Through my rearview mirror, I watched Kang park his navy blue Crown Vic behind me. As he walked over to my vehicle, I rolled my window down. "I don't see any movement in any of the windows. I wonder if anybody is home."

"Doesn't matter. I have a 'sneak and peek' warrant. Nobody needs to be home."

Kang and I hurried over to the tong. "What made you think to do that?" I asked.

"I swung by yesterday and sat out front for a few hours. No one came or went. In fact, the tong looked how it looks now: vacant."

When we reached the entrance, Kang removed a small leather case from the pocket inside of his suit jacket.

"Your own set of tools. I'm impressed," I said.

Kang flashed me a smile before he went to work. The lock on the front door was a single-cylinder deadbolt, not the most effective at keeping people out. Kang had the door unlocked in under a minute.

Once inside, we could easily see that the reception area and the small informational library were both empty. The lights were off, but enough sunlight shone through the windows that we didn't need to turn them on. We listened for a minute or so and heard nothing suggesting anybody was there. Still, we drew our weapons and climbed up the stairs.

On the second floor, we stared at an empty recreation room. The lights were off, but again the area was sunlit. The pillows on the three sofas were neatly in place. The magazines on the coffee table in the center were still in the fanned-out position I had remembered seeing them in a few days ago.

Off to the side were two teak tables with green felt tops—typical for mahjong games. I didn't see any game pieces lying around, though. We searched the kitchen. No dirty dishes in the sink. I turned the faucet on, and water spurted before settling into a stream. A sign it had not been used in a while. *Strange.*

Of the two offices on the floor, one was outfitted with everything an office would need: a desk with an executive leather chair, a filing cabinet, and a bookshelf lined with various Chinese-language books. I checked the filing cabinet. It was empty. So were the desk drawers. Aside from a yellow pad with a pen lying on top of it, I saw nothing else to indicate any sort of administrative work had taken place there. The other office was furnished with a table and a few chairs; maybe it served as a meeting room.

"Kyle, you thinking what I'm thinking?"

"Yup. This tong might have turned over a new leaf, but it's still rotten."

Our discovery had me gripping the handle of my Glock a bit tighter and wishing I had my bulletproof vest strapped on.

We approached the roped-off stairwell and listened once more before heading up. Kang unhooked the rope and led the way, hugging the wall. Before reaching the landing, we saw that the third floor was darker than the others. Kang peered over the top step. "It looks empty," he whispered.

It was.

A large, empty space made up the third floor. There was a closed door to the left. I covered the stairs while Kang moved ahead. Our priority had switched from searching the building to clearing it. We had to be sure we were the only ones there. After a quick check, he whispered back to me, "It's an empty closet."

There were a couple of drape-covered windows facing the street. Kang moved the drapes to the side to let in the sunlight. It made all the difference.

I led the way to the next floor, hugging the wall of the narrow stairwell. The steps were wooden but surprisingly quiet. I expected creaking on every step but heard none. The fourth floor was also dark, but I could see a scattering of mismatched furniture and a few banker boxes stacked against the far wall. Kang covered the stairs as I cleared the area.

We continued up to the top floor. I stuck with the lead. Right away I noticed a difference. First, it was smaller— more like an attic space. Second, it wasn't dark like the two other floors. Third, someone lived there.

Chapter 8

"Kyle."

"I see it." Kang moved up next to me.

The open space had a slanted ceiling, the highest point being in the middle, maybe a fifteen-foot clearance. A single window with no drapes was positioned directly opposite the stairs. The walls were bare, as was most of the space. Pushed against the left wall we saw a single-mattress bed with a thin white comforter draped over it. There was a nightstand with a small bed lamp. A ceramic teacup and teapot sat on the linoleum floor next to it.

I walked over to the bed, and my nose picked up a faint but familiar scent of jasmine. Tea was my first thought— maybe incense—but I didn't see any ashes or stick remains lying around.

"I wonder if the caretaker of the tong lives here," Kang mused. "It's not much."

Aside from the teapot, cup, and a few empty food packages, there were no other personal items that I could see. The place looked more like a crash pad than a home. We both holstered our weapons.

On the other side of the room, tucked in a corner, was a

small washbasin with a mirror hanging on the wall above it. A half-filled bottle of water sat on the counter. There was a door next to the basin. I pushed it open and saw a single toilet with a roll of toilet paper on the rung. *Someone's using it.*

I turned around and saw Kang fiddling with the small drawer on the nightstand. "Anything in there?"

He shook his head. "Just an old gum wrapper." He walked over to the single window and pushed it open. "That's interesting. It was partly open. Every other window in this place had been sealed shut."

"Maybe that's how whoever lives here comes and goes." I chuckled.

Kang placed a hand on either side of the windowsill and braced himself before leaning out. "Well, the fire escape is below, so it's plausible." He pulled himself back in and brushed off his hands. "I still think the front door and stairs are a better way up here."

We didn't discover the silver bullet I had hoped we would find, but we had a new lead. "We need to talk to the person calling this place home."

"I agree." Kang raised his arm and wiggled it so his jacket sleeve fell back and revealed a silver watch. "It's a little after nine thirty. It's strange that no one is here."

"Do tongs keep normal business hours?"

"Sure. It's here for their members, but maybe there's business happening off-site. Though this living space doesn't surprise me." He glanced around the room. "Could be one of the members crashes here if it's late and they're too tired to go home."

Little by little, I felt as though we were ruling out the tong altogether.

"But this is interesting." Kang reached down and picked up the porcelain pot with a blue hand-painted design. "You see this pattern? It may look like your typical blue-and-white ware, but if I'm not mistaken..." He turned the pot around and looked at the bottom. "Ah."

"What?" I asked, stepping closer for a better look.

"You see these four Chinese characters? They are the marking of Kangxi, an emperor who ruled during the seventeenth century. Since the porcelain still retains a remarkable whiteness and the cobalt hasn't lost much of its blue hue, it could be real. If so, it would be worth a lot." He lifted the top open, stuck his nose inside, and then shrugged.

"It looks old to me."

Kang laughed. "The Chinese are masters at forgery. Sometimes all it takes to age a piece is rubbing animal urine over it to dull the shine. I'll have Ethel take a look at it. She's much more knowledgeable on Qing Dynasty pottery than I am."

"That's impossible."

Kang chuckled at my joke, but his depth of knowledge on Chinese culture and history was staggering.

"What's that mean to the investigation?"

He shrugged. "Not sure, but I want to study the design. I've never seen anything like it before. Usually pottery depicts the countryside—you know, mountains, rivers, temples, the occasional crane. But this one, it shows a person moving along the rooftops of what looks like a village. It may be nothing, but I want to look into it." He removed his phone and started snapping pictures before deciding he would just temporarily borrow the pot. "I'll return it later."

We swept each floor on the way back down but found nothing that could tell us more about the mastermind or pinpoint his whereabouts.

As we exited the tong, Kang used his tools to relock the deadbolt. "We were never here."

I looked up and down the quiet lane, wondering if anyone might have seen us enter or exit the tong. "Maybe you should ask Ethel if she can put us in touch with the person who manages this place. I'd like to officially question them. There might be more to that room on the top floor."

"Good idea."

I watched Kang drive off before I got into my car. I sat still for a moment eyeing the tong once more. Did a connection exist, or had I simply fabricated one? As I turned the key in the ignition, movement to my left caught my attention. An elderly man with a toothy smile stood next to my vehicle. He was hunched over, not so that he could look inside but because he had a hunchback. A white cane supported his weight. I hit the passenger window button. "Can I help you?"

His smile disappeared. He backed away, shaking his head, and hobbled off. "Wait, I want to talk to you." I shut the vehicle off and quickly caught up with him in a few steps. "What do you know about the people in that tong?"

"I know nothing." He avoided making eye contact and kept walking.

I followed him. "You sure? Seems like you might see a lot of things around here. What do you know about the Hop Sing Tong? Seen anything strange happening over there?"

"Not see anything," he said before disappearing through the entranceway to an apartment building almost directly across from the tong. If he had a street-side apartment, he would have a direct view of the goings-on of the tong all day and night. Just as I gripped the doorknob to go after him, Reilly rang my cell.

"Abby, did the search turn up anything?"

"Nothing concrete."

"My contact at the CIA has information on your girl. Get here and I'll brief you."

I wavered for a moment, but prodding the old guy for information would have to wait. I spun around and headed back to my vehicle.

Chapter 9

Kang couldn't believe his luck—an open parking spot right outside the CCBA. Heck, a parking space anywhere on Stockton Street was a rarity.

He parked his vehicle on the busy street that bordered the western end of Chinatown and fished out three quarters from the ashtray. *That should be more than enough for the meter*, he thought as he grabbed the paper bag holding the teapot he had taken from the tong.

The façade of the CCBA was typical Chinatown architecture; red tiles populated the gabled rooftop with sweeping corners and continued onto the balcony walls and the overhang at the entrance. Two large stone lions sandwiched each side of the granite steps leading to the entrance, and four gold, squared columns with Chinese lettering engraved on them stood evenly spaced at the top of the steps.

Kang waved at the elderly woman who sat behind the reception desk. "Hi, Grace. Is Ethel around?" Gold-framed reading glasses sat at the edge of her nose, and she wore the same short, permed hairdo he remembered seeing the first day they had met.

"She's in her office," she said with a smile and a tilt of her head.

"Thanks." Kang was a familiar sight at the CCBA and, unlike most visitors, didn't need to be escorted or announced. He continued past Grace without slowing and made his way down the short hall to the last office, stopping at the entrance.

Ethel Wu sat behind a large, glass-topped desk wearing her signature pair of black cat-eye glasses. She was on the phone but peered over the rims at Kang, motioning for him to take a seat in one of the two brown leather guest chairs.

Kang tried to ignore the conversation, but Ethel had a voice that cut through most anything. Though he could only hear one side of the discussion, he gathered it had something to do with the upcoming elections.

Ethel was a common fixture among the city officials who represented the district that included Chinatown. It was a known fact that those politicians relied heavily on her support. Almost all of Chinatown voted in step with her. Kang often teased her about running for a city council seat. She replied that she was perfectly happy at the CCBA and had no political aspirations.

Kang busied himself by admiring the large landscape mural on the left wall of her office. It was the Li River twisting its way around pointy karst peaks poking through early morning fog. A local artist had painted the mural more than ten years ago.

"You never tire of looking at it, do you?" Ethel said, dropping the phone receiver into its cradle. She removed her glasses and held them in her hand.

"It's beautiful. One of these days, I'll get over to that part of the country."

"Better hurry before you're dead." Ethel bounced in her seat with laughter. "So what brings you here today?"

Kang removed the teapot from the bag and placed it on Ethel's desk. "What can you tell me about this?"

Ethel's head leaned forward. Her eyes narrowed into slivers as she placed her glasses back on her nose. Her gaze shot up at Kang for a brief second before settling back on the teapot. "May I?" she asked, motioning to the pot with her hands.

"Sure."

Ethel picked up the piece and slowly turned it around, taking in every detail of the design. While looking at it, she made tiny acknowledgements and nodded. Eventually she held the lid down and turned the pot over to its side, revealing the painted characters on the bottom. No sooner had she seen them than she took a deep breath. "Do you know what this is?"

"I'm guessing it's from the Qing Dynasty."

Ethel peered once more over the rim of her glasses. "That's right." She gently placed the pot back on the table. "I'm pretty sure this isn't a fake. Of course, the only way to truly know is by drilling a small sample of powder from the piece and heating it. The more it glows, the older it is. On the low end, it could be worth three hundred bucks, but it looks to be in decent condition. High end might be about a grand."

"Determining its authenticity and value isn't the only reason why I brought it to you." Kang pointed at the pot. "I've never seen a design like that before. It's atypical."

Ethel nodded. "It is, isn't it?" She leaned back and placed her hands on her lap. "Where did you say you got this from?"

"I didn't. The owner is a friend," Kang lied. "He found it in his mother's attic, buried inside an old footlocker, and was curious to know its worth."

"I can only guesstimate its value at this stage, but this design—I've seen it once before."

Kang's eyes widened. "Where?"

"When I was young, just a small girl, I used to rummage through my father's personal items. Tucked away in his desk were a couple of paintings on parchment. I remember one of them had a similar picture."

"Did you ever find out more about it?"

"Not really. All I know is that his father gave the paintings to him; he'd gotten them from *his* father."

"Family heirlooms?"

"You could say that."

"You wouldn't happen to have those paintings, would you?"

Ethel shook her head. "I have no idea what happened to them. I'm sorry I can't be of any more help."

"Maybe there's no special reason behind the design; it's just a man walking on rooftops and nothing more." Kang picked up the teapot and placed it back into the bag. "Thanks for your time. Always appreciated." Kang stood and walked around the desk to give Ethel a hug.

"If you find out anything else about the pot, let me know," Ethel said.

"Will do."

Kang sat quietly in the driver's seat of his car as he examined the teapot. His hope that it would provide a much-needed boost to the investigation had died back in Ethel's office. *Maybe I'm the one that's making this more than what it really is.* Kang placed the teapot on the passenger seat and started his car. He couldn't help but feel hopeless at that moment. His partner and friend was in danger. Short of sticking by her side twenty-four hours a day, Kang wasn't sure if his actions were doing much to help.

Chapter 10

After twenty minutes of stop-and-go traffic, I arrived at the Phillip Burton Federal Building. I had the elevator to myself and counted along with the numbers to the thirteenth floor. Before heading into Reilly's office, I made a detour to the break room. Even though I was eager to hear the information he had, I wanted to be prepared for what I expected to be an in-depth briefing. That meant having my hands wrapped around a warm mug of my favorite tea.

I found Reilly sitting in his leather executive chair and jotting notes in a spiral notebook. Stacks of yellow manila folders covered his desk. The metal blinds on his window were slanted down, obscuring the northern view of the city. I cleared my throat, causing him to jump a little.

"Abby," he said as he looked up and closed the notebook. "Thanks for your promptness. Take a seat."

"I thought the CIA didn't share information." I made myself comfortable in the chair opposite his oak desk.

"Our friendship goes way back." Reilly handed me a yellow Post-It note that had a phone number written on it.

"I thought you had information."

"I do unofficially. He's an operations officer in the

Special Activities Division. Spent the last five years conducting top-level operations in Asia."

The job title conjured up images of the spy activity that Hollywood loved to perpetuate. I imagined Reilly's contact was one of those agents that the U.S. government would deny having any knowledge of should any crap hit any fan. Could explain why he only gave me a phone number.

"Make the call. Shred the note." Without saying another word, Reilly opened his notebook and resumed writing.

I stared at the number as I left his office. *Who are you, and how can you help me?* When I reached my desk, I made the call.

"Yes?" said a male voice, followed by silence.

There had been a time when the CIA switchboard was noted for answering their phones by simply repeating the number. That practice was long ago shelved, and now they at least said, "CIA." But a simple "Yes" I wasn't expecting, and I was thrown just a little by the starkness of the call.

"This is Agent Abby Kane with the Federal Bureau of Investigation. I was told you could help me."

"Sorry, I didn't recognize the number. Did Meredith fill you in?"

"There is no Meredith. Would you like me to provide a DNA sample?"

"I needed to be sure of your identity. Reilly speaks highly of you."

"I'm glad he conveyed that information."

"Meet me at two p.m. outside your building. There's a hotdog cart."

"I know it."

"Look for the guy with three dogs."

Before I could answer, I heard a click, and the line went dead.

Time passed slowly as I waited. I kept busy by once again looking over the information that Choi, my protégée, had forwarded to me. There wasn't much. Mostly it was a few mentions of Sei in a couple of reports. Choi assured me that the girl I was talking about was the girl in those reports. The evidence was hearsay, but it was all I had. Sei wasn't a POI, so the fact that she even made it into a report was surprising. The most useful of all the intel was an actual sighting of her in Shanghai by an officer as opposed to an eyewitness.

At a quarter to, I locked my purse in the lower filing cabinet of my desk, threw my matching suit jacket on, and proceeded to the rendezvous point.

One hotdog cart existed near my building, and it was near the southeast corner of the block. Just outside the south entrance of the building was a large open area. Roughly fifty feet of concrete expanse separated the front doors and the street. It wasn't worker friendly, as there weren't many places to sit, and tree coverage only existed along the curb.

I slowed my steps as I scanned the area looking for a

guy with three hotdogs. I didn't see anyone matching that description. *Well, I guess I'll head over to the cart.* I started in that direction, focused on the short man, Pepe, who had been serving up the grass-fed beef weenies for as long as I had worked for the FBI. A man in a suit stood in front of the cart, but I didn't peg him as my contact; he wouldn't be dressed that way.

A short perimeter wall, maybe two feet tall, wrapped the corner of the block. People often sat there while eating lunch. I spotted a man dressed in jeans and a dark blue hoodie wearing a black skullcap and wrap-around Oakley shades. He was halfway through a hotdog. Even though I didn't see two more, I had a feeling he was my guy.

"You got one for me?" I asked as I approached him.

He flashed a bright smile as he handed me a white paper bag. He was human. Inside were two more. I grabbed one of the silver-wrapped morsels and took a seat next to him.

"Hope you like them loaded."

"Is there any other way to eat them?"

He shoved the last bite into his mouth and brushed his hands while I started in on mine.

"Sorry about the covert runaround. I just got back two weeks ago. My Jedi senses are still operating at field level."

"Does it ever stop?"

"Not really," he said with a chuckle. He stuck his hand out. "The name's John Park."

"Nice to meet you. Reilly tells me you spent time in Asia."

"Almost all of my assignments take place there. I just completed an operation in Shanghai and am due a little R&R. I have family in San Francisco. The timing worked out for you."

I swallowed. "I'll say."

He motioned to the bag between us with his eyes.

"Go for it. I'm good with one."

He started in on the third dog. "This girl you're asking about, I know a little about her. She's not on the agency's radar, but most of what I discover isn't."

"Explains why I'm having trouble finding information on her. Do you want to know what I know?"

"Not necessary," he said, flattening the paper bag next to him and placing the half-eaten dog on it. He reached into the front pocket of his jeans and fiddled around before stopping and standing up. He shoved his hand back into his pocket and pulled out a USB hard drive. "Everything I know about her, including a few photos, is on this."

"You have photos?" I asked, rising to my feet and taking the mini hard drive from him. I was eager to get back to the office and look over the goods.

He nodded. "I had been tracking a local judge. An informant told me he would be meeting with a high-ranking Triad member. Turns out I had bad intel. The meet was between your girl and the gang member. I snapped photos anyway."

"Did you—"

"Everything I know is in the report. I hope it helps." He sat back down and picked up the remaining half of his dog. At the same time, I dropped the hard drive and bent down to pick it up.

From the corner of my eye, I saw Park's hotdog hit the ground. When I looked up, he was slumped over to his side, and half his forehead was missing.

Chapter 11

I never heard the first gunshot.

However, a second bullet whizzed by my face and hooked my attention, fast. I took another look at Park. There wasn't anything I could do for him. Bleeding out wasn't a concern; he was dead before he hit the ground.

I dived over the perimeter wall just as another bullet struck it, spraying chips of concrete into the air, which rained down upon me. I brushed my hair out of my face and blinked a few specs of dust out of my eyes. All around me people sought cover in an area that was as sparse as they came. I poked my head up, and another bullet sent it back down.

My ears told me that the shooter was using a sound suppressor, but still the pops were audible and, by my estimate, came from the west. My best guess was that he had holed up in the residential building at the other end of the block. I highly doubted he had hunkered down in one of the surrounding government buildings. If I were right, the sniper would be just over 300 yards away. *He's trained. He should have hit me.*

I had my weapon drawn, but it was no match for a

high-powered rifle. Considering the timing between shots, it was bolt action. Had it been semiautomatic, I probably would have been lying next to Park. The shooter had fired four rounds, more than enough for him know he had compromised his position.

I peeked over the wall again. No more shots. He was on the run. I leapt to my feet and used the cover of the young maple trees that lined the street to move forward. Other agents were filing out of the entrance of the federal building.·

"The shots came from that three-story building," I called out, pointing. "We need to contain. I don't think the shooter has made it out yet."

There were six of us advancing. Off in the distance, I heard the wail of sirens closing in on our position—only a matter of time before the area would be swarming with SFPD. This guy was toast.

When we reached the building, three of us positioned ourselves outside the front entrance. The other three circled around toward the back. The front entrance was a security gate composed of eighteen-gauge welded steel bars running the length. A small area housing a bank of mailboxes provided a buffer to a windowed door. Aside from being buzzed in, there wasn't a quick way to access the building.

More agents appeared, Reilly being one of them. "What's the situation?"

"Sniper fire directed at Park and me came from this

building. Park's body is at the southeast side of the federal building. There was nothing I could do."

"Damn!" Reilly's jawline tightened as he took a quick moment. "Is the shooter still inside?"

"As far as we know. There are three agents covering the back."

"Got it. Stay here. Do not breach the building."

Reilly assumed command and ordered the agents with him to set up a perimeter. He then met with the first units from the SFPD that had arrived on the scene. I knew he would work to lock down the surrounding blocks.

"I'm circling the building," I told the two agents next to me.

"We were ordered to stay put," said Walter Bennett, one of the agents with me.

I looked back at him. "We need to be one hundred percent certain this guy hasn't already slipped out."

"How do you plan to do that?"

"I don't know, but it beats standing here and doing nothing." I kept my eyes trained on the roof as I moved alongside the front of the building. A typical metal fire escape clung to the front exterior like an ugly birthmark. "Keep an eye on that," I shouted to the agents near the entrance.

At the end of the building was a walkway no wider than five feet that separated it from the adjacent building. Smooth stucco walls rose on either side. I kept my eyes fixed upward as I moved through the narrow passage. *No way the shooter could climb down. I don't even see a window.* That was when I saw someone leap from one building to the next.

"He's on the rooftop," I shouted, backing out of the walkway. I followed along the sidewalk and pointed. "He's up on top, heading north." I continued in that direction, stopping only to look down another narrow walkway. I caught sight of his left leg just as he cleared the gap. He wore camouflage pants. How clichéd.

He had two more buildings he could traverse before running out of rooftops. At that point the shooter would have to loop back or work his way down. I passed the next and final walkway but didn't see him. By then, Bennett had caught up. "Head down this pathway in case he loops back. I'll cover the other side of the building." I picked up the pace and headed for the end of the block. When I got there, I saw no fire escape, but I also had the sun beaming at an angle that affected my sightline with the rooftop. *Where are you?*

I peeked back around the corner, looking for Bennett. He was out of sight in the walkway. "Bennett, he's not here," I called out. "Do you have eyes on him?"

"Negative," I heard him shout back.

I moved along the building, wondering if he could cross over to the adjacent building to the west, but a lane between the buildings made it too far to jump. However, there was another fire escape, and my shooter was making his way down.

We laid eyes on each other at the same time. His arm rose, and I dashed behind a dumpster just as he squeezed off a round. He had ditched the rifle for a handgun. I popped up and fired two rounds. The stairwell deflected both. I ducked back down, but there was no return fire. I peeked around the dumpster. Once again, I saw his weapon trained in my direction. A wild shot chipped the asphalt to the right of me.

The magazine in my Glock 22 had thirteen rounds remaining—more than enough to get the job done. If I could catch him while he was descending the stairs away from me, I would have a clean shot when he made the turn and headed down the stairs that faced me.

I took another look and saw his back. I trained the sights of my weapon, my arm steadied by the cover over the dumpster. There would be no discussion. No warning. No nothing. I had one objective.

Three steps. Two steps. One step. Turn. *Bam!*

The shooter's body crumpled and rolled end over end down the stairwell until it came to rest on the platform, his gun falling to the pavement below and bouncing to a stop. He looked unconscious. Or dead. I had put two rounds into his chest—always enough to drop a man, not always enough to instantly kill him. I kept my gun trained on him as I walked over to the fire escape. A tickle of sweat ran down the side of my face, and I could feel a slight strain in my blouse as it stuck to my back. It wasn't so much a sign that I was hot but more of an indication that I had just taken a life.

The *plat, plat* sound caught my ear before my eyes noticed the red drops painting the asphalt directly under the shooter.

Bennett arrived shortly after with a few other agents. "Kane, you all right?"

"I am. He's not." I motioned upward with my head as I stepped away from the falling drops and holstered my weapon.

One of the agents put a call in for medical support while I gave Bennett the lowdown of what had happened after we'd parted.

"We got lucky on this one," he said, resting both hands on his hips, his dark blue jacket pushed back.

No, this was me being good at my job.

"He almost got away."

Aren't you glad I came to work today?

Reilly arrived shortly after, and his forehead appeared very disappointed in me. "Did you not hear me earlier when I said to stay put?"

"I heard you."

He shook his head and pulled me off to the side. "You disobey another direct order from me and I won't hesitate to slap you with an insubordination write-up," he said, his voice low and direct. "You hearing that?"

"Understood."

As I brought Reilly up to speed, his eyes told me I had made the right call to look for our shooter. But I understood his frustration and reasoning. I had defied a direct order from him in front of other agents.

Reilly raised his hand above his head, blocking out the sunlight, as he sought a better look at the body. A crowd of looky-loos had already gathered, and most had their phones out to document. Reilly glanced over at them. "It's news before the news." His eyes fell on me, but before he could get another word out, an object fell to the pavement near us—a smartphone.

"It must have fallen out of his pocket," I said, walking over to it. The phone was encased in a heavy-duty yellow protector. The screen was cracked, but we could clearly see what was on it—the log-on page for the Chasing Chinatown game. The player was Team Militant.

It had begun.

Chapter 12

"Those shots… they were intended for you," Reilly said as his hand covered his mouth.

I opened mine, but nothing came out. I didn't know what to say. One of the players had actually taken up the mastermind's offer. The hit on me had become a reality.

While procedures had been put into place to ensure my safety, most of my coworkers, Reilly included, didn't think one of those knuckleheads would actually come after an FBI agent. And yet twenty feet above me, warm blood dripped from a body.

I guess I'd bought into the hype as well. I had always known it was a possibility but had wanted to believe that it wouldn't happen. It was like having a hunch the tooth fairy wasn't real and then being crushed when it proved to be true. Denial had overcome me. I didn't want to accept the truth.

If I had ever had a surreal moment, well, that was it.

I knew there were people all around me; I could hear different voices. I even heard Reilly call out to Bennett, "I want a team analyzing the information on that phone pronto. Find out who this guy is."

But it felt far away, unbelievable, like Neverland.

Is this really happening? Over and over the thought churned in my head. My head had dropped, and my gaze was lost when I felt pressure on my arm. "Maybe there's only one idiot playing the game," Reilly said. His voice was soft, calm, hopeful.

I wanted to believe that this guy was the anomaly, but my gut disagreed. "Park was innocent," I said. "He didn't deserve to die."

"It's not your fault, Abby."

"I remember dropping the USB drive. I bent down to get it. That's when he was hit. He was behind me, sitting on the wall. My forehead was the target."

"Abby, we'll do everything possible to protect you and your family."

My eyes shot back to Reilly. He already knew what I had been thinking.

"Castro and Lin are good agents. Your family is safe, but I'll put a few extra men on the detail until we can sort through what we're up against."

The arrival of CSI caught Reilly's attention. "Look, Abby, I don't think you should go home just yet. Team Militant might have other players. They probably don't know about your family or where you live. We can't compromise that."

I wanted to go home, but the agent in me agreed with Reilly. This wacko could have come after me at my home—

it would have been to his advantage—but he didn't. "I want the family moved to another location."

Reilly nodded. "Done." He spun on his feet and disappeared into the chaos.

All around me, a team of agents and police officers moved to secure the immediate area. No one in. No one out. We had to control the scene and determine whether our shooter had used a partner or acted alone. There could be others.

An agent from the bureau approached me holding a bulletproof vest. "You should put this on."

Most of the agents I worked with, whether I knew them or not, were aware of my situation. I had been a little defensive at first with all the extra attention. I felt like the little sister the big brothers were looking out for. But still, I saw the silver lining: I had an army of federal agents watching my back.

I thanked him and took the vest. I wore a simple paddle holster that day, so I removed my suit jacket and slipped the vest over me. I had a form-fitting jacket, so there was no chance of putting it back on. I carried it in the crook of my arm.

As I secured the vest straps, a familiar voice drew my attention. I turned and saw Kang walking in my direction. The Civic Center didn't fall under the Central Precinct's jurisdiction. He had gone out of his way.

"Abby, I came as soon as I heard. What the hell

happened?"

I looked up at the fire escape that now had a body tent secured around it. "Team Militant is what happened."

"You mean an actual player came after you?"

I had to laugh, because even "Cautious Kang" hadn't thought one of the teams would make a move on me. I relayed the day's events to him. His furrowed brow and periodic nods only further reinforced the seriousness of the situation.

"The first shot dropped a contact Reilly had put me in touch with, a CIA agent."

"CIA? Sheesh." Kang turned his head away briefly. "This story gets more unbelievable."

"I'm the lucky one."

"That's the other body at the corner of Turk and Golden Gate?"

I nodded. "It's unfortunate. He had no beef in this."

"What was the meet about?"

"Park was an operations officer who had spent time in Asia, particularly Shanghai. The hope was that he would have actionable intel on our assassin. The information I received from Choi had last placed her there."

"And?" Kang raised both palms.

I retrieved the USB flash drive Park had given me from my pants pocket. "He handed me this right before he got clipped. According to him, it holds everything he knows about the girl."

"That's hopeful."

"Yeah, in a roundabout way. I mean, tracking down a ghost assassin in order to shut the game down so that its players, who I can't identify, won't come after me is, well, grasping." Even I saw that what I was attempting was pretty absurd.

"What about the shooter? What do you know about him so far?"

"Aside from his team name, not much. He had no identification on him, but we're running his prints and looking into the room he rented for his operation."

"Kane."

I turned to the voice behind me and saw Bennett approaching. "Our shooter turned up on the National Crime Center database." Bennett removed a small notebook from his jacket. "His name is Colin Benton. A passport scan had him arriving in the U.S. via Seattle from Vancouver."

"He's Canadian?" I asked.

"Negative. He's an American. Last known address was in North Dakota."

"I never suspected an American team," I said. "What else you got?"

"He did four years in the army. He was a qualified marksman but was dishonorably discharged for an unauthorized kill during Desert Storm."

"Well, that explains his ability to take out a target from a few hundred yards away. He should have hit me as well."

"There's more," Bennett said. "He has known ties to a small militia group that the Bureau had been keeping tabs on. They called themselves American Freedom and operated in Montana. They had a growing presence until the leader was arrested and later found guilty of pedophilia. They disbanded shortly after."

"This keeps getting better." Kang folded his arms across his chest.

Bennett continued. "This Colin guy tried to start his own outfit with some of the remaining AF members, but it never gained traction. He went off the grid shortly after and hasn't been seen since."

"Until now," I said, shifting my weight from one foot to the other.

"You know, the Vancouver destination isn't that far away," Kang added. "Did you know a team was active there?"

"According to the game, no."

"Maybe it stopped tracking teams."

"It didn't appear that way the last time I logged on, but you might be right. Team Militant should have been listed as being active in that city unless he hadn't completed an Attraction."

"We should log on and check to see if there's any movement with the other teams. Maybe it's a glitch."

I shrugged and tilted my head. "Either way, I think we have to assume that all fourteen teams will come after me."

"Why? Because this guy did?"

"No. It's something that I've thought all along but tried to suppress. My bounty isn't a bonus Attraction. It's the only Attraction. If the players want to remain in the game, they have no choice but to come after me."

Chapter 13

News choppers circled above while their counterparts operated media stations at the north end of the lane. The high-powered lights used by the cameramen lit the area as puppet reporters all fed their stations the same story. This would be a spectacle that would continue long into the night and provide days of fodder for the ratings-starved media outlets. They were making Team Militant infamous.

"Are you stuck here all night?" Kang asked.

"No, but I'm waiting for word on where my family is being relocated to."

No sooner had I said that than my cell phone rang. It was Castro. He said they were in the process of relocating my family and they were safe.

"I want to see them."

"I'm sorry, Abby, but we don't know if you're being watched right now, and—"

"No, I'm sorry, because that's not how it's going to work," I countered with a voice that was stern but even toned. I needed Castro to understand my position without unnecessary explanation. "I know if I'm being tailed or not. Give me the address."

"What was that about?" Kang asked after I ended the call.

"The agent in charge of moving my family to another location thought it was best that I not be in contact with them right now. Worried about me being tailed."

"He doesn't know you that well." Kang chuckled. "Where are they?"

"Heading to Napa Valley—a small B&B."

Kang pushed his bottom lip up and mulled over my answer. "That works. Is that where you're going now?"

"I'll swing by the house first for some personal items, maybe a quick shower."

"Who's there?"

"Nobody. It's empty."

"Tell you what." Kang clasped his hands together. "I'll come with you."

I patted the front of my vest. "Thanks, but I'll be okay."

"That wasn't a suggestion," he said, flashing a grin. "Come on, I'll follow you with my car."

Before heading back home, I wanted to fetch my purse and laptop from the office. I had been keen on seeing if there was a glitch in the game or if I perhaps no longer had access to live updates. When Kang and I exited the alleyway, we did our best to avoid the media gauntlet.

I kept my head down and worked to make my body look as inconspicuous as possible, but it didn't help. The shrill I had come to recognize as the coming of the beast had sounded. *No, it can't be.* I looked over to my left, and my jaw fell limp. Striding toward us dressed in a white pantsuit with matching heels and a cherry-red scarf was my nemesis, Suzi Zhang.

She had her black, silky hair pulled around to the left of her neck, resting over her perky breast like a Pantene shampoo commercial. Each step crossed over in front of her, accenting the swing of her hips from side to side. *Why can't you just walk normally and not like you're trying out for a spot on* America's Next Top Model? It annoyed me the way she turned the sidewalk into her catwalk.

I had first met Suzi in a hospital when she came to visit Kang. We had gotten off on the wrong foot, and it stayed that way.

"Agent Kane, might I have a moment?" she called out, microphone in hand and white veneers on display. *And what's with using the "might"? You're Chinese, not British.* I rolled my eyes and kept walking until Kang answered.

"Sure, we have a moment." He turned to me. "Is that okay?"

No. Not okay. "I guess."

Kang and I waited as Suzi positioned herself next to me, checked her makeup, raked her fingers through her hair a few times, and flashed a few practiced smiles before giving her cameraman the go-ahead. I just stared at her bared chest, wondering about the blouse that should have been accompanying her suit.

"This is Suzi Zhang reporting live from the Civic Center, where a deadly sniper shooting has taken place. Standing next to me is FBI Agent Abigail Kane."

Abigail?

"As we understand, you were the initial target of the lone gunman. Could you tell us why you were singled out?"

"There's no indication that I was the target, nor have we come to any conclusion on whether the gunman worked alone or conspired with others." *I'll contradict every question you ask, so keep wasting everyone's time.*

"But isn't it true that you are being targeted by a group of killers?"

I shot a look at Kang before turning back to her. "The FBI has no knowledge of a group of killers that are targeting agents," I said, tucking my shoulder-length black hair behind my ears. "As far as the bureau is concerned, this is an isolated incident, and we are investigating it as such. That's all the information I have at this time. Thank you."

Before the serpent could spit out another question, I kicked my tiny legs into gear and exited the frame. Once we were out of range of any sort of recording device, I laid into Kang.

"I can't believe you told her about my situation," I said, picking up the pace.

Kang kept in step and raised both hands in protest. "I swear I didn't say anything. I never discuss my investigations with her."

"Really?" My left eyebrow arched, punctuating my question.

"Look, Abby. She's a journalist—"

"Journalist? That's being generous."

"Look, my point is that she probably heard a few sound bites from my phone conversations with you and dug around a bit. I'll be more mindful around her from now on."

My gut told me Kang spoke the truth, but somehow his girlfriend had put two and two together, because no other media outlet had suspected that I had been the intended target. And I didn't think asking me those questions had anything to do with her doing her job. I think she wanted to let me know that she knew or at least give the impression that she knew what was happening. Speaking to me was about exhibiting control. *Bitch!*

We arrived at my home forty-five minutes later. Kang parked his Crown Vic across the street, and I pulled my Charger into the driveway.

I was halfway to the front door before Kang exited his vehicle. "I'll be in and out," I shouted as I held up a hand.

Once inside, I flipped a lamp on near the front door, and an empty living room stared back at me. I tried to recall the last time I had come home to a quiet house, and the answer was never. No bear hugs from my youngest. No tantalizing smells from the kitchen to tease my nose and water my mouth. Nothing. I suddenly felt lonely. I shook off the dullness before it could settle in.

I hurried up the stairs and down the hall. My eyes had adjusted to the dark, and there was enough moonlight shining through the window at the opposite end of the hall that I didn't bother switching on the hallway light.

I pushed opened the door to my bedroom, hit the light switch, and did a double take. The floral comforter on my bed had disappeared, and the marigold-colored sheet had been replaced with a stark white one. Near the bottom of my bed, folded in a neat square, sat a gray woolen blanket. Next to it I saw a long-sleeved blue denim shirt with a number stenciled across the left breast. It looked like a prison uniform. But the strangest thing was the crudely constructed rubber mask lying on one of the pillows. The hair had been glued on in clumps, and the facial features were drawn on with a black marker pen.

And then I heard it—slight movement behind me— before the bedroom went dark.

Chapter 14

Not again.

I took a step while turning, hoping to set distance between myself and whomever I was about to face. At the same time, my hand shot to my side holster, but I had lost the draw. A foot separated the barrel of a gun from my nose. Behind it was a shadowy figure, not much taller than me and a little on the thin side. Boxing this guy into submission was an option.

"Remove your hand from that gun," he said with a noticeable accent.

I followed his instructions while I estimated the distance between my right foot and his crotch. *Damn you, short legs.* I still had my vest on, but at this distance, my face was an easy target.

I wished I hadn't told Kang to stay put. Maybe that punk would have gotten the jump on both of us. I doubted it. Kang would have waited downstairs.

"You know why I'm here."

"Is that a question?" I asked.

"You answer. I ask. Are we clear?"

"You're playing the game."

"I'll be rich soon. You do realize that, don't you?"

The situation grew dimmer with each passing second. I had yet to see an opportunity to turn it around. "I do."

"They made it easy. No riddles, no clues. But we do have a theme: San Francisco movies. That's the fun part."

*The rooftop sniper—*Dirty Harry—*that's why he targeted me at work.* "So now what?"

"You asked another question, but I'll forgive your incompetence." He took a step back toward the door. "Put on that shirt." He motioned with the handgun.

There was enough moonlight shining into my bedroom that I could make out some of my assailant's features. His skin was dark, an olive complexion, and he spoke with a South American accent. He was clean shaven and bald on top, or maybe it was shaved as well. It didn't matter. He wore a dark peacoat, the type the inmates from *Escape from Alcatraz* wore. Maybe that had been his way to get into character—an inmate taking out another inmate.

I grabbed the shirt off the bed. To my surprise, it was fairly close to my size. I unbuttoned it and slipped an arm through one of the sleeves when he stopped me.

"Vest off."

"I think it'll fit if I still have it on," I said, feigning naiveté.

"You're making me angry."

I removed the vest, revealing the black blouse I wore. The holster housing my department-issued Glock was still securely tucked into the waist of my pants. "Should I remove this as well?"

He steadied his arm. "Take it out slowly. Toss it over there."

I did as he said. "You know my partner is just outside."

"He's not your real partner. Don't call him that."

"Oh?" I said, slipping an arm through one sleeve of the uniform.

"He works for the San Francisco Police Department. You work for the FBI. You're working together, but you're not really partners."

Semantics.

"And what makes you think *I* don't have someone outside with a gun pointed at the back of your cop friend's head? Do you really think I've been able to take the lives of twenty-six people without careful planning?"

"I don't believe you killed that many people."

"Of course you don't. The police—not even the FBI—want to admit they can't catch someone like me. You people are so stupid. You can't catch anybody."

His arrogance pissed me off. It made me want to charge forward and put everything I had behind a punch to his face. But that thought also made me realize something else: He hadn't killed me yet. He could have killed me first then slipped the shirt on me, put the mask over my head, and recreated his little scene for his photo, but he hadn't. That told me he needed or wanted me alive. Or maybe he simply didn't want to dirty his hands. *What are you planning, and how can I exploit it?*

He reached into one of the front pockets of his jacket and removed something. It wasn't until he threw the object and it landed on my bed that I realized it was a pair of handcuffs.

"Put them on," he said.

I could sense a smile in his voice, but I wasn't about to give up so easily. "No."

"What did you say?" He straightened up—shoulders back and chest popped out a bit.

The way I saw it, this guy couldn't have been watching me for very long. He had to have arrived in San Francisco recently, maybe a day or two ago. "I think you're working alone," I said, changing the subject.

"You don't know what you're talking about."

"I think you're afraid of me, of what I'm capable of."

"That's not true."

From his reaction, I could tell there had been some truth to what I had said. "You don't have a plan. You got lucky," I continued.

"You stupid bitch. Look at the prison shirt, the blanket, the mask. That's planning."

"No, that's equipment."

I didn't buy what he tried to portray: a serial killer. First off, the way he spoke, his thought process—it didn't come across as someone with a high IQ like Ted Kaczynski or Jeffrey Dahmer. He was more street thug. Simplistic. Sure, he had some sort of plan, but the details weren't there. He'd had an idea that he had been figuring out along the way. A true serial killer would have controlled the situation and his victims from the very start whether they knew it or not. He didn't have control of my movements or my mouth. In fact, with every second that I remained free, I gained the upper hand.

"Pull that trigger, and in this quiet little neighborhood that gunshot will sound like a bomb exploding. You'll then need a minute or two to finalize your plan. No photo. No money. The only exits out of this house are on the first floor. I'm guessing you entered through the backdoor, since the front hadn't been breached. A thick hedge encircles the entire backyard, making the narrow passageways on either side of the house your only viable escape route, but you already know that. Of course, with the valuable time you'll waste documenting your efforts, you'll most likely run into my partner as you're making your way down the stairs while he's entering the house. I doubt you're working with someone else, so in the end, it'll be a spirited competition of who can react faster and with more pointed accuracy."

He opened his mouth to speak, but I continued.

"You're not like the other players. You don't derive a thrill from the kill. You stumbled across this game and saw an opportunity to make a quick buck. You're an opportunist, and that's why you won't win. You're playing the game for all the wrong reasons," I said, taking a step toward him.

I had guessed right. I had him questioning and wondering how I could be so accurate in my assessment. His arm relaxed briefly before he straightened it.

"What's the matter, the gun too heavy? You've never pointed one at someone for this long, have you?" I took another step forward.

"You have no idea what you're talking about. Your psychological lecture won't work on me. Save it for someone else. Wait, there won't be another time."

He laughed.

I struck.

I shot forward, my shoulder squared with his groin, knocking him back and off his feet. The jolt to his body had the effect I had hoped for. His gun had fired. *Come on, Kyle. Get your butt up here.*

I sat up and slid across his chest. I shoved my right leg into the crook of his neck while using the other to pin his right hand down so I could grab his gun. My surprise move had him immobilized. The question was, for how long? I expected him to buck me off at any second, but instead, he squirmed under me like a little boy unsure of what to do. I had a sneaking suspicion he was nothing but a bully who thrived on picking fights with people who appeared weaker than he. *You picked the wrong person.*

Eventually, I knew he would come to his senses and

fight back. I also kept expecting to hear the front door open, followed by the pounding footsteps of my partner making his way up the stairs. Nothing.

I took a chance and released my right hand from his. Raising my arm up high, I drove my elbow into his right cheek. I repeated the move. I had meant to break his face on the first try.

The blow sent him into a fury. He shot his hips up with enough force and sent me flying over his head.

I flipped over as soon as I landed. So did he. He brought his gun around. I kicked my left leg out. My heel blasted his face, snapping his head back and shaking the gun loose from his grip. I continued with a volley of cycle kicks that fought to slow his climb forward.

One by one, he wrapped his arms around my legs and pinned them beneath his chest. A smirk stretched across his pockmarked face as he crawled forward. "You're dead, bitch."

I propped myself up on my elbows and pushed away, but it was too late. He swung his left arm around toward my head.

I looked up and found Kang staring at me. "What happened?" I asked while sitting up. The room spun, so I lay back down.

"I was about to ask you the same thing. I heard a gunshot. When I got here, you were knocked out cold, and this guy had a broken neck," he said with a head toss.

Broken neck? I looked at the motionless body next to me. His head was tilted my way unnaturally, and his eyes were open, but I saw no life flowing from them. *How?* "The last thing I remember was kicking him in the face while he threw wild punches."

"Maybe one of your kicks did him in."

"I don't see how... Wait. You said you found me unconscious?"

"Yeah." Kang pulled out his cell phone and called for backup and an ambulance.

In the meantime, I replayed the events of the night in my head. I definitely remembered kicking my attacker in the head and face. Maybe I did get lucky. I have decent leg strength. He wasn't a big guy—certainly plausible. As I lay there wrestling with my thoughts, a cool draft rushed across my face. I looked over at my bedroom window and saw the drapes fluttering in the breeze. That window had been closed earlier.

Chapter 15

Two hours after Kang had woken me up in my hallway, CSI wrapped up their portion of the investigation and allowed the medical examiner, Timothy Green, to remove the body.

Green and I had known each other for a few years. We had worked a couple of cases together and shared coffee once or twice. As head of the San Francisco Medical Examiner's office, he almost never came out to a crime scene, but I suspected his decision to make an appearance had a lot to do with my being involved.

He had arrived wearing brown corduroys and a yellow and green T-shirt promoting medical marijuana. He had a moppy mess of brown hair with a scattering of white on his head. His left ear was still pierced, but the tiny diamond stud had been replaced with a black barb. The light patchouli scent I associated with him permeated the air around him. There was no mistaking that Green was more hippy than hip, and most would crinkle their brow upon hearing that he was the city's chief medical examiner.

"I'm sorry they kept the body here for so long," he said, adjusting the wire-framed spectacles on his nose. He spoke calmly and softly, as he always did.

I waved it off. "I know the drill."

He smiled. "Yes, you do. Such the pragmatist." His gray eyes lingered on mine longer than most would. I didn't mind the attention, but I was mindful of keeping our friendship just that.

"I hope I'm not prying, but I overheard your conversation with Detective Kang earlier. Are you in some sort of danger?"

I pondered his question briefly before answering. Broadcasting my situation had been the last thing I wanted to do. I didn't need to help the Suzi Zhangs of the world. "I'm chasing someone, and they don't like it. They're doing everything they can to stop me."

"Is that what happened here?" He gave the crime scene a quick once-over. "You're telling me this guy was sent after you?"

I nodded. "There may be more." I decided to fill Green in on the details of the night and its connection to the Chasing Chinatown game. "We found the game app on his phone, and he had been logged into the game as Team Favela. We don't know his true identity yet."

Green took a deep breath and blinked his eyes repeatedly. "I don't know what to say, Abby. This is serious. You could be attacked *again* at any moment."

Just then, Kang appeared. "I just got word that the department will increase patrols on your street."

"Increased patrolling? How is that supposed to keep her safe?" Green blurted. His raised tone even took me by surprise.

Kang towered above Green much as he did me. With his hands pocketed in his blue slacks, he turned toward the man who had boldly questioned him. "It's called having a presence. It'll serve as a deterrent."

"Oh, well, in that case, Abby should be much safer, because apparently an officer in a passing vehicle is much more of a deterrent than an officer sitting in a parked car across the street."

Ooh, a direct attack. This wasn't the first time I had witnessed the alpha posturing between the two. I knew they had history, but Kang had never filled me in on the details. I guessed it had something to do with the crush Green had on me.

With his neck craned back, Green showed no sign of backing off. In fact, he had leaned in, mostly to keep the conversation away from the other ears around us. My brain told me, *Break up the little boys before it goes any further.* But my ego countered, *No, not yet. It makes me feel sooooo good.* Maturity prevailed.

I stepped between the two. "Timothy, I appreciate your concern. You're a good friend. Let me know what you find with the autopsy." I steered him toward the stairs but disguised it as friendly pats on the back.

I watched Green descend the stairs and walk out the

front door before turning back to Kang, who had a smug look on his face. "You happy?"

"I don't know what you're talking about," he said, briefly looking away. "Look, in light of the situation, I think I should drive you up to Napa. You're still heading there, right?"

"She's not going anywhere." We both turned to find Reilly making his way up the stairs. "We can't risk you compromising the safe house. You'll have to wait a little longer."

"Wait, that's not the deal."

"I realize that, but the situation has changed. Anybody you come into contact with could be a potential player of the game. I'm locking you down right here, right now," he said. "And that's nonnegotiable."

Reilly had done what I had feared he would do since that day the mastermind placed a bounty on my head: He had handcuffed me within my own investigation. "How am I to do my job?"

"Where there's a will, there's a way."

"This case won't solve itself," I continued.

Reilly looked at Kang. "Good thing you have a partner to help out."

I let out a loud breath. "How long are you making me stay in my room?" I folded my arms across my chest and shifted my weight.

Reilly had both hands resting on his waist. He seemed

at ease with his decision and undeterred by my sarcasm. "We'll play it by day. I've assigned two agents to provide a security detail: Logan Knox and Steven Copeland. They're familiarizing themselves with the property as we speak. You can introduce yourself to them later."

"I really don't think—"

"Abby, they'll be under strict orders to make sure you remain here. If you need to come in to the office, they'll escort you. But you have access to the NCIC database, and all of your files are on the office server. You should be fine working from home. Is there anything else I should know?"

Earlier, on the phone, I had filled Reilly in on what had taken place, but he had still insisted on coming over. He walked a little way down the hall, looking at the mess the CSI team had left. "I know a good crime scene cleanup crew," he said as he turned and headed toward the stairs. "I'll have them stop by tomorrow. The Bureau will cover the cost."

"The lock on the back door is punched out," I said in a huff.

"Add that to the tally." His words faded, and that was the end of the conversation. I had become a prisoner in my home and, as far as I was concerned, an even easier target.

Chapter 16

Kang offered to spend the night. In fact, he insisted. I was too tired to fight him, and my head still throbbed from the smacking it had taken earlier. The two agents who were assigned to me had already appropriated the guest room for their sleep shifts. Lucy still had a youth bed, which wouldn't work. Po Po's was a queen, but Kang said he would feel better if he were on the same floor as me. That left Ryan's room.

"I appreciate everything you're doing, but—"

"I know, I know. You can take care of yourself, and there are two other agents on the premises," he said. "But I want to do this."

"What about your girlfriend? Won't she mind?"

"She'll have to understand. This is work, not a teenage sleepover."

I opened the door to Ryan's room. He had a double-sized bed with a navy-blue comforter and matching pillows. He had shed his Godzilla-themed bedding shortly after our move to the U.S.

Two Bruce Lee posters hung on the wall, along with a judo instructional poster that demonstrated forty techniques.

His gi hung on the doorknob to his closet. A six-drawer dresser stood next to a wooden desk and chair. A low bookshelf housed his growing collection of martial arts books, a lava lamp, and a realistic figurine of Bruce Lee complete with yellow jumpsuit and black nunchucks.

Ryan had grown up fast over the last year or so. The toys of his earlier childhood were gone, replaced with a small flat-screen TV, a PlayStation 3, and a laptop. A skateboard stood upright in the corner, and glow-in-the-dark stars adorned the ceiling of his room.

"Looks like your boy has really taken an interest in the martial arts."

"He's been taking judo for a while and recently started with kung fu lessons. I take him to the gym with me when I can to teach him a few of my own tricks." I flashed Kang a smile.

"I should spar with him one day."

"That's really nice of you. He would like that. Kung fu is where his real interest lies."

"Does he still call you Abby?"

"Most of the time. Every now and then he'll slip and say the 'M' word."

"That's gotta make you happy."

"You know, I get it; he was old enough to remember his mother when she passed."

"He'll come around."

I removed a few pieces of clothing from the bed. "You

should be comfortable here."

Kang nodded.

I let out a yawn as I exited Ryan's room. "If you want a shower, there are fresh towels in the hallway cabinet. Help yourself."

"Abby," Kyle called out before I entered my bedroom, "we only briefly discussed this, but everyone, including your boss, seems to think a kick is what broke your attacker's neck."

"Maybe I did do it. We'll see what the autopsy turns up."

"But the open window—how sure are you of it?" he said, walking toward me.

I looked at the still-open window. CSI had dusted it for fingerprints but found none. "Pretty sure, but I guess I could be wrong. Maybe I opened it when I got home and don't remember." I shrugged.

Kang slipped by me and walked over to the window. He stuck his head out and looked around before pulling it back in. "There's nothing for anyone to crawl down on, but the jump to the grass below isn't terribly high. It's possible to land without tweaking an ankle. Did the CSI crew check outside for prints?"

"Yeah, they didn't find any. They also got up on the roof but didn't find any noticeable disturbances, as they put it, but that doesn't mean anything. Even a skilled burglar can avoid leaving a trail."

Kang shut the window.

"So now *you're* thinking there was another person?" Up until that point, I had been the only one buying the second-person theory.

"The odds of you kicking him and breaking his neck at the exact same moment he knocks you out, well, I think you'll have better odds with a lottery ticket."

I crossed my arms across my chest and leaned against the doorframe. "Okay, say there was a second person. Why would they break my attacker's neck and then flee the scene?"

"Competition? Another team wanted a crack at you?"

"Another team? Interesting, but why not then finish me off? The job's halfway done. Why wait and then have to make another attempt?"

"Maybe they had a different plan. You talked about a theme earlier—movies that take place in San Francisco."

I thought about what Kang had said. There could be a little truth in it, especially if the other team's gratification for killing stemmed from a very specific act or procedure. "We're stretching, but let's continue. Say this other team arrives here after us. They would have to enter my home without alerting you, my attacker, or me, right?"

Kang nodded.

"Only then to discover that they were too late when they see that Team Favela has already engaged me. Again, this happens without alerting either one of us."

"Or they got here before we did, saw the other team, and decided to wait it out."

"Eh, I feel like if they did arrive before us and spotted Team Favela, they would have either left or taken out the other team."

"But then there's a body unless they attacked them in the backyard. Doesn't seem likely, though."

"I agree. Still it all feels very Silly Putty to me... You know what it could be? Maybe he did have a partner, and that partner got greedy."

"Still, why not kill you, snap the picture, and be done with it?"

We were chasing our tails, grasping at anything to make the second-person theory work. None of it did. We had talked ourselves into an empty corner. I yawned again and looked at my watch. It was nearing midnight. "Let's continue this conversation later."

"Good idea. Rest might bring us a bit of clarity."

After parting with Kang, I opted for a quick shower instead of the lingering bath I had been thinking of. Thirty minutes later, I was under my covers, makeup free, with minty fresh breath courtesy of a thirty-second burning gargle.

I don't know how long I had been asleep, but I remember opening my eyes briefly as I turned over to my side. That was when I saw movement. At least, that was what I thought it was. I had already closed my eyes when I mulled that thought.

Was that movement a shadow from the tree branch outside?

Were the drapes drawn over the window before you went to bed?

I'm pretty sure they were. That would disqualify the tree.

Eye floaters?

Now that's a likely culprit.

Were your eyes open long enough to register them?

Hmmm, good question.

Why not open your eyes and take a look?

Why? Because I don't think I can stomach yet a third attack in one day.

So if you keep your eyes closed, somehow whoever is in your room will disappear?

Wait, at what point did we graduate to someone being inside my bedroom?

There's only one way to find out, right?

I opened my eyes and didn't see anything, but my window was open. Again.

Chapter 17

I sat up in bed and stared at the window. I was pretty sure Kang had closed it earlier. I was certain it was shut before I slipped under the covers. And yet there it was, open, with the curtains flapping in the breeze.

I slid my legs over to the side of the bed and stood up. I usually slept in the buff, but seeing as there were three men under my roof whom I wasn't in a relationship with, the conservative part of me had me sleeping in a light tank top and cotton athletic shorts.

I walked over to the window and moved one of the curtains off to the side for a better look outside. The nightly fog was absent, so my adjusted eyes fared better in the darkness. I looked down at the single-sloped roof of the enclosed patio. The lights were off, and I heard nothing, but I assumed one of the agents was sitting inside there.

I scanned the yard, not looking for anything in particular. Or maybe I was—a reason for my window to be open. I shifted my eyes over to the top of the tall pine tree and slowly traced downward the outline of the trunk and its arched branches. One of the branches, a straggler, jutted out close to the house about a foot to the left of my window. I had thought of hiring a landscaping service to trim it but had never gotten around to doing it. I stared at it, wondering what a trim would cost. That was when I saw a slight movement in the tree.

I blinked my eyes and leaned out the window a bit. I had already questioned my memory, and my imagination seemed to be getting the best of me, but dammit if I wasn't sure I had seen something un-tree-like move.

The dark shape moved again. This time it wasn't brief; it slowly traversed along the branch toward me. It was too big to be a raccoon. I could see that much. It stopped just as a slice of moonlight beamed down in front of it. Out of the patch of darkness and into the light, a hand appeared. I swear it looked as though it waved at me.

In an instant, I drew a sharp breath, and the knock of my heartbeat slammed against my chest. I spun around and reached for my holster that lay on top of my dresser. As I drew my weapon, I turned back toward the window, but the mysterious person had disappeared. I knew then that I wasn't imagining things.

I darted out of my bedroom and down the hall. "Kyle!" I shouted as I approached Ryan's room. I pounded the door twice as I passed by. "Someone's in the tree!"

I didn't bother waiting for a response and continued down the stairs. By the time I rounded the corner at the bottom, I saw that a light had been turned on toward the back of the house. Past the living room and through the dining room I continued until I hit the small hallway that led past the kitchen, Po Po's room, and the guest room. Agent Knox stood near the door that opened up to the enclosed patio.

"What the hell?" He had his knees bent slightly and his hand near his side holster, ready to draw. His eyes were opened wide, a little buggy looking and blinking excessively as if he had been sharply woken from a deep sleep. Maybe he had fallen asleep on his watch. Or maybe it was because I was running toward him with my weapon drawn.

"Someone is in the tree. Move! Move!"

Knox spun and headed back into the patio. I ran past the guest room as the door opened. It was the other agent, Copeland. "Contain the front of the house!"

I grabbed the Maglite I kept in a small niche near the door and followed Knox into the backyard, flipping the switch for the lightbulb above the doorway. It helped a little.

I switched the Maglite on and held it in my left hand. My weapon rested on my wrist so the sights were aligned with the strong beam of light. "I saw someone on that branch," I called out as I panned the light across it. Knox moved to secure the backyard, his weapon out front.

By then, Kang had appeared. He raised his weapon up to the tree, following the path of the flashlight. "What's the situation?"

"I saw someone crouching on that limb."

Kang looked around. "Where's the other agent?"

"The front of the house," I said.

Kang headed to the front of the house.

I continued to shine the light on the limb where I had seen the movement as well as the surrounding ones, but I knew whoever had been there had already disappeared. I helped Knox search the thick hedge, thinking maybe that person had managed to reach it and squeezed inside before we reached the backyard. Nothing.

We moved to the front of the house, and I spotted the outline of a tall person standing on the sidewalk. Copeland had height like Kang, but he also had a good amount of meat on his body—the opposite of Kang's lanky physique. He turned as he heard our approach.

"The front of the house is clear. Detective Kang headed right, up the street," he motioned with his thumb.

There was only one streetlight in that direction, leaving the area fairly dark—a likely direction for escape.

"You know I have to ask," Knox started.

"I saw someone. I'm not imagining it." I spoke fast. The thumping in my chest continued.

"Okay, that's a problem. The property was breached without our knowledge."

I looked Knox straight in the eye. "I think that person was in my room."

I filled them both in on what had transpired upstairs.

Copeland opened his mouth first. "I'll check for any signs of a forced entry." He moved to search the exterior of the house.

The back door couldn't be locked thanks to Team Favela's break-in earlier. I sensed Knox had the same thought running through his head.

"It's possible that door was used as an entry point while I performed a perimeter walk, but I doubt it. How could this person have known the lock was broken?" Knox pointed up toward the house. "Are there locks on those windows?"

Almost all of the original windows on the Victorian were double hung and equipped with a simple sash lock. Most wouldn't open because they were painted shut, but I had cracked the coat covering mine when we first moved in. I liked fresh air. "They do. I can't remember if Kyle locked mine when he shut it. I normally don't since I'm on the second floor so…"

"Do you really think someone was in your room?"

I shrugged. "Pretty sure. I mean, maybe it might have been floaters I saw or a shadow from outside. What I do know is that someone was in that tree. I clearly saw a hand in the moonlight."

"So maybe you woke just as this person tried to access your room. They got as far as opening the window then had to retreat."

Why didn't Castro catch that branch as an entry point

into the house? "That's possible. Maybe it's another team playing the game."

Kang had reappeared, slightly out of breath. "I searched all the way to the end of the block and didn't see anyone."

We brought Kang up to speed on our conversation. He confirmed that he hadn't locked the window.

"Great. Seems like everyone caught the same flight to San Francisco." Kang shook his head and let a defeated breath flap his lips.

"I know, right? Seems like that increased jackpot lit a fire under their butts."

"Safe to say this person has been here long enough to know that was your bedroom," Knox said. "Who knows how long he or she has been watching you, waiting for the right opportunity?"

"What are the odds that three teams would strike on the same day?" Copeland asked no one in particular.

"One Attraction. Winner takes all. That's why," I said, looking at him. "It's a race. They don't have the luxury of sitting back and taking their time."

Knox scrutinized the houses across the street. "You're not safe here," he said, turning toward me. "These people know where you live. We'll need to move you."

"He's right, Abby," Kang said. "We don't know who these teams are or what they look like. Anybody who comes in contact with you is a potential threat."

"Hey, hey, let's not overreact. All we need to do is adjust." I held my palms out. "We know they'll come here, so it's easier to stay put. I know my neighbors and am familiar with all the faces on this street. If I move to another location, it creates more unknowns. It'll be harder to spot a threat."

The group fell silent for a moment.

"All right," Knox said, "we'll do it your way." He placed a hand on my shoulder and gave it a soft squeeze. "I pray I never have to tell you, 'I told you so.'"

Chapter 18

The sun had just begun to rise and peer through the sheer curtains that dressed the double-paned window in the small bedroom when bladder pressure in Zoric's abdomen woke him. He rubbed the crust from his eyes and looked at the slender woman next to him. She was turned away, lying partially on her side and stomach. Her chestnut hair fanned across her creamy bare back. The white comforter only covered her up to her waist, where a tattoo of a unicorn on her lower back peeked out.

Her name was Adrijana Lilic, and she had always been by Zoric's side until a year ago when they both fled Serbia separately. Zoric had been a high-ranking member of the Zemun Clan gang in Belgrade. The recently elected mayor had put the gang in his sights and vowed to eradicate their presence in the capital city. Zoric had no interest in seeing how determined the elected official was to demonstrate to his constituents his commitment to being tough on crime. He thought it best that he and Adrijana stay apart temporarily. Adrijana went west to the small town of Pristina in Kosovo while he and Petrovic fled east to Chisinau in Moldova.

He pulled the comforter up over her shoulders; the morning temperature outside had to be in the low teens, and it was not much warmer in the room. Even in the hottest month of summer, the mercury never rose above 65 degrees Fahrenheit.

Zoric slid his feet over the edge of the double bed and stood. He walked quietly across the cold tile floors, hugging himself for warmth. His half-erect penis swung with each step. He would wake Adrijana after he took a piss.

A few steps out of the bedroom, near the door to the toilet, Zoric stopped and peered into the living room. Tucked under a woolen blanket and sleeping soundly on an old futon was Petrovic. He had an arm resting across his eyes, shielding them from the penetrating light of the rising sun. He still wore his grungy boots.

They had arrived at Adrijana's apartment about a week ago. It was the only place Zoric thought they could be relatively safe and lie low. Killing those Greeks in Thessaloniki had been stupid, and he knew it. This hadn't been the first time his lack of patience had gotten him in trouble. It had been a constant his whole life.

"One of these days, you'll get us killed," Petrovic would say to him.

Zoric would always reply, "Not today."

Zoric had calmed Petrovic's fears of retaliation by coming up with a plan. Well, it wasn't much of a plan; mostly it involved convincing Adrijana to part with her stash of cash that he knew she always kept hidden from him. They could use that money to pay for their travel to San Francisco and continue playing the game. It was the only real solution they had. Plus, it would put them out of reach of the Greeks, and if they won, they could then go anywhere in the world.

However, there was a contingency—one Petrovic wouldn't like—that Adrijana had laid down for funding their expedition west: Team Balkan would have a new member, and the take would be split three ways.

Chapter 19

Adaira Kilduff stared out the window of the seventh-floor hotel room located in San Francisco's financial district. She particularly loved that hotel, having stayed once before. It wasn't that the room was well appointed or that the hotel had outstanding customer service or that the amenities were top notch; no, it had actually been fairly lackluster in all departments. But what she had discovered during her last visit was a discreet way she could come and go without raising an eyebrow with the front desk staff.

If she entered the stairwell from the second floor and made her way to the ground level, a door opened into a small hallway that led to another door that opened into the pub next door. From all sides, the door looked as though it led to an unremarkable broom closet, so the only people who trafficked the corridor were hotel employees fulfilling in-room dining orders. The doors were never locked, and the pub was always busy.

She had been in town for two days and was aware of Team Militant's unsuccessful attempt at fulfilling the game's singular Attraction. The sniper shooting topped every news broadcast, though none of the media mentioned the game or the alias used by the gunman. That told her they had no clue or the FBI had issued a gag order. Either way, it worked in her favor. Team Militant just came off as a nutty, one-man militia bent on sticking it to the U.S. government, and the game was free to continue.

Adaira had already figured out where Agent Kane lived and still hadn't decided if attacking her there was a viable option. If a heavy security detail were present, it would be problematic. Adaira wasn't a bust-down-the-door-and-shoot-'em-up kind of person. Her victims in the past had been people she knew, most of them intimately. It allowed her to plot out every step, to think through every repercussion that could arise from the act. It was the real reason she had gotten away with her previous murders.

This method, however, slowed her advancement in the game. So far, she had sacrificed two of her pay pigs for the game. Their generosity had been waning, and she didn't think she'd lost much by disposing of them.

Adaira had always thought she hadn't been right for the game and had seriously thought about dropping out because of the difficulty of finding victims, not to mention the themed kills required by the game, but the draw of the prize was too much to ignore. She had to try. With the latest change in the game dynamics, Adaira had become much more hopeful. "One kill and the winner takes all" gave her an honest chance at winning.

A swoosh of water could be heard coming from the

bathroom before the door opened. Out walked a stocky woman with a buzz cut. Her face was adorned with a labret, a nasal septum piercing, and a third-eye piercing, and her earlobes were stretched and outfitted with black flesh tunnels.

She wore a white button-down shirt that she was busy tucking into the waistband of her slung jeans. A pair of black combat boots anchored the ensemble. The sleeves were rolled up to her elbows, revealing tribal tattooing on her forearms. Inked right below the knuckles of her right hand was the word BORN. On the other hand was the word BUTCH.

Adaira turned around and smiled. She had met Alex in an after-hours club during her last visit to the city. Alex had taken a liking to Adaira, and the bulldog had quickly become a puppy following her around during her stay. Adaira cozied up to the butch boi and learned that she had a questionable past that included a stretch of time in the Central California Women's Facility for burglary, the illegal sale of firearms, and unintentional manslaughter. "Unintentional" was Alex's take on the incident.

Adaira's gut had told her to stay clear, but it was that very thing about Alex that kept her engaged. That, and every now and then, Adaira enjoyed being piledriven by a dyke.

"So, babe, what's the plan?" Alex took a swig from an open bottle of Jack Daniel's before wrapping her arms around the tall redhead and sucking on her neck.

Adaira pulled back immediately. "No marks. Remember?"

"Man, I'm just trying to snack on you."

"You can snack, just not there."

A crooked smile formed on Alex's face, revealing her nicotine-stained teeth. "I know what you want." She flicked her tongue like a serpent before dropping to her knees.

Adaira leaned back against the window, turning her head sideways to admire the city lights once again. The fog was minimal that night. To the south was the Embarcadero Center, whose four buildings were outlined with lights year round. To the north, in the direction of the Golden Gate Bridge, was North Beach's camel hump: Telegraph Hill. Protruding from the very top of it like an icy-blue glow stick was the famous Coit Tower. It was always beautifully illuminated at night, with exterior lighting that changed to suit the city's tastes. The last time Adaira was in town, the tower had been drenched in orange to celebrate the San Francisco Giants' win of the World Series.

Adaira rested both hands on Alex's head, gently guiding her. She had yet to figure out a workable, themed kill for the game, but she had enlisted a sidekick. Adaira was well aware that she hadn't the means to kill Agent Kane the way she needed to, but she knew Alex could. Convincing her to go along couldn't have been any easier, and Adaira didn't even have to mention the game. She simply told Alex that the FBI agent had been working with Scottish authorities to have her extradited back to Scotland, and if that happened, Alex could forget about eating her ever again.

That's all Alex needed to hear. "Man, fuck that bitch. She ain't taking what's mine."

The question about a plan that Alex had asked earlier was not without reason; Adaira had yet to come up with one. She needed an idea that complied with the game's theme. She knew she wanted a movie that represented the essence of Team Kitty Kat, one that was equally thrilling as being a dominatrix.

The first film that came to mind was *Doctor Dolittle.* She had remembered a scene in which Jake the Tiger was contemplating suicide from the top of Coit Tower. Adaira thought of how fun it would be if the lady agent leapt or was pushed from the tower. However, the movie didn't quite meet her expectations. Family fun wasn't exactly what she'd had in mind.

Not being a huge movie buff, Adaira was forced to do a search online, where she found an article that listed every movie shot in the city. *Escape from Alcatraz* jumped out at her, as she was certain it would be a thrill to watch Agent Kane try to escape her grasp. But then she came across the erotic thriller *Basic Instinct.* It seemed almost too perfect. She was exactly like the lead character: intelligent, sexy, deadly. But in the end, Adaira chose a movie that had a driving scene that appeared to be as equally thrilling as whipping a man into submission.

Chapter 20

Two days had passed without incident. Neither my neighbors nor the media were the wiser of what had been taking place at the House of Kane. I had talked Reilly out of setting up a command post on my front lawn. That would have drawn unnecessary attention and freaked out the neighbors.

An agent at the bureau had dug up information on Team Favela. The man's name was Antonio Rocha—a wannabe thug from Rocinha, one of the larger slums of Rio de Janeiro. His background proved interesting.

Apparently, his mother was a powerful woman in the *favela* where he grew up on account of her longtime boyfriend, Francisco Sá Silva, the right-hand man of one of Rio's most feared drug lords. Sá Silva was said to have helped her raise Rocha since he was ten. I suspected Rocha never quite lived up to his expectations. Maybe playing this game was his way of proving himself to the man he called Dad.

According to the game, Team Favela should have been in Buenos Aires, Argentina. There were no waypoints on the map connecting that city with another, so I could only assume B.A. had been his first crack at the game. As far as I could tell, he had only completed one of the Attractions before the objectives of the game had changed. *They're only a flight away.*

I exited the back door, looking to find Knox. He'd already had the lock on it fixed and reinforced; in fact, all entry points into the house had been refitted with extra security fixtures. The floodlights were also operational again. My neighbors would just have to deal with it.

Knox had set up two live animal traps in the far corners of the yard in an effort to keep the raccoons from triggering the security lights. "It'll help to eliminate a false trip." He motioned upward with his eyes to the lights.

I studied the wire mesh cage. "What'll you do if you catch one?"

"We'll have animal control come out and relocate it."

I took a deep breath of fresh air and kicked a pinecone that had fallen from the tree. Last Thanksgiving, Lucy had collected enough for her entire class to make pinecone turkeys. Lucy had made one for each of us, and they served as the centerpieces for our festive dinner. Remembering that day made my stomach turn; I had yet to see my family since the night they had been whisked away. I continued to push Reilly for a visit, but he rejected my request each time. He had me contemplating a decision that would not make him happy.

In the meantime, video calls provided the best option.

At least I could see my children. Ryan and Lucy didn't seem too bothered by what had happened. They had been separated from me before. Castro and Lin were doing a great job at keeping them entertained with movie rentals and video games. A homeschool teacher, cleared by the bureau, had been hired to provide schooling since they weren't allowed to attend.

Ryan's only complaint had been that he missed his judo and kung fu classes. "Abby, I try to practice my moves in my room, but it's not the same. I don't have an opponent to spar with."

"Have you tried asking Agent Castro or Lin if they can help you train?"

"Yeah, but they're always too busy doing what they do, or Po Po is making them drive her someplace."

"What about outside? Are there things to do?"

"There's a small vineyard where I sometimes play hide-and-seek with Lucy, but we can't go too far. Oh, Mr. Fulton is teaching me about wine."

Ed and Betty Fulton were the owners of the B&B. They were high school sweethearts who had gotten married and stayed that way. They'd been running the B&B ever since Ed retired from the Navy.

"Well, that sounds interesting. No sampling!"

Ryan laughed. "Abby, I have to know if I made it right. Don't worry; Mr. Fulton told me I'm supposed to spit it out. It tastes yucky anyway."

Po Po appeared content with the temporary arrangement because of the fact that the B&B had a larger and better-equipped kitchen than I had been able to provide her with. Lin had the duty of driving her to Chinatown every other day. The payoff had been healthy weight gain for the two agents. I, on the other hand, had lost a few pounds.

I had left Knox and retreated to my cove on the third level of the house when Kang called.

"You know that teapot I took from the tong?"

"Yeah," I said, easing myself down into my leather chair.

"Did I leave it at your house by chance?"

"Don't tell me you lost it."

"I might have. I had it with me that night you were attacked. I left it in my car."

I crossed my legs and doodled on the notepad lying on my desk. "Did you search your car?"

"Yeah, it wasn't there. Then I thought I had taken it into my place. I tore the house upside down but nothing."

"What about—"

"I already grilled Suzi. She was my first go-to."

"Aside from the fact that you lifted it from a place you shouldn't have, is it a big deal if you don't find it?"

"Yes and no. I won't bother you with the details."

"Bother me." I recrossed my legs and added hooker heels and long hair to the stick figure I had drawn.

Kang told me about the meeting he'd had with Ethel regarding the teapot.

"So that thing could be worth a lot of money?" I drew a microphone in the hand of my stick figure reporter. "I'll look around. Maybe you brought it inside."

"That's not the only reason; I still think that design on it has meaning. I showed it to my friend Ethel. She had seen something similar before—drawings her dad had—but she didn't know what it meant. Luckily, I still have those pictures I snapped of the teapot while we were there. I can study those."

I filled in the speech bubble above my little stick figure. *This is Sushi Zhang reporting live from Nob Hill where word is a mysterious person is not picking up after their dog.* "Okay, well, let me know if anything comes of it."

"I will. By the way, how are you holding up?"

"Meh, I'm okay. I haven't had any real reason to leave the house except wanting to see the kids and Po Po."

"No-go there?"

"Nada."

"Look, if you need anything at all or if there's something I can do for you, let me know. I'm serious."

"Be careful. You're giving me a whole lot of leeway."

Kang chuckled. "What doesn't kill you makes you stronger. Isn't that the saying?"

I hung up thinking about the investigation and how it

had dropped Kang and me into a series of absurd situations. He had become someone I could depend on without fail, someone I could trust with my life, someone I still had a stupid little crush on. I blamed it all on that day when he first saved my life. *Stupid hero-crush syndrome.* That's all it was.

I opened the window above my desk and gazed outside. It was two thirty in the afternoon. I knew because, across the street, I watched our postwoman make her way from house to house. She had that familiar navy blue bag slung over her shoulder, and as always, she wore a sky-blue, short-sleeved shirt and gray culottes. Rarely did I ever see her in trousers, even when it rained. The temperature outside hovered in the low seventies. Not too cold but not too warm. I guess all the walking she did helped.

Near her, a black squirrel scurried down a telephone pole and contemplated crossing over to my side. It retreated when a forest green Mustang approached; its throaty engine cut through the hum of my neighbor's lawnmower.

Copeland caught my eye just as I pulled back from the window. I stopped and watched him walk down the driveway to the edge of the sidewalk, where he surveyed the street in both directions. On his way back to the porch, he gave me a two-finger salute.

I smiled at him and wondered how I might give him and Knox the slip so I could visit my family. Kang's generosity had planted a seed in my head.

Chapter 21

That night after dinner—spaghetti, veal meatballs, antipasto salad, and garlic bread ordered from Fanelli's Deli—I bade goodnight to Copeland and Knox and headed upstairs. I wanted to take another look at the information on the USB drive that Park had given me. While I had combed through it carefully the day after the sniper shooting, I hadn't seen anything as being helpful with locating Sei or even telling me more about her.

The hard drive contained a few surveillance photos of the meeting Park had mentioned. There were a bunch taken of the Triad gang member sitting at a sidewalk table outside a small coffee shop and a few more of Sei standing at the table. The rest were of the two sitting and talking. Most of the photographs had her wearing large sunglasses, but Park managed to take one when she briefly removed them to scratch her cheek. I was thankful he had gotten that shot. Without it, I couldn't have confirmed that the woman in the pictures was Sei. The odd thing about that one photo was that it looked as if she had been staring straight into the lens, as if she knew someone was photographing her.

Also included was a report Park had written about the

death of an informant in a Shanghai short-time love hotel. On the night the hotel manager discovered the dead body in the room, security cameras attached to the hotel's exterior captured a person dropping down from a fire escape in the alley next to it. It was only when the person passed under the camera that they became recognizable due to a bright, yellow glare from a nearby neon sign. It was a woman who looked a lot like Sei.

She had the same long, straight, black hair and slender but firm physique that I remembered from my encounters with her in Bangkok. Her outfit was a form-fitting jumpsuit. While Park might have thought she resembled the woman from his other pictures, I was on the fence; the video footage was grainy. I thought Kang might help confirm whether it was Sei since he had also interacted with her.

Park's report went on to note that the informant was an aide to the judge. I guessed the judge found out about this guy's loose lips and had somebody silence them. Both upper and lower appendages were removed from the victim's face.

I replayed the video, pausing it at the instant the neon glow drenched the woman. It seemed as though her eyes were looking straight into the camera. I couldn't be sure because of the video quality, but it looked that way. If this woman really were Sei, was she simply exhibiting narcissistic behavior, or had she been baiting whomever would investigate the informant's death to catch her?

All cues pointed to Sei being the mystery woman, but Park had nothing concrete tying the woman in the video to his informant's death except that she used the fire escape to exit the hotel. His report stated that they never found out who did it. I wasn't sure how much time Park had spent developing that asset, but the depth of the investigation told me it hadn't been a huge loss.

There were a few other reports involving dead people in which eyewitnesses described a similar woman being seen in the area: small, slender, and wearing a black jumpsuit.

Did she always wear that outfit when she executed someone? Could it be an extension of her personality? Was it associated with a gang or an organization she belonged to? I had never seen an outfit like that during any of my Triad investigations. *It could be a Chinese thing, but I doubt it.* I was probably overthinking the outfit, but I took a snapshot of the paused video anyway and emailed it to Kang. *Maybe the professor has an opinion on this.*

I had honestly begun to think all the hours spent investigating her were amounting to nothing more than a monumental time-suck. But I knew the only way to the mastermind was through others, and getting to them had proved difficult to say the least. For the first time in my law enforcement career, I feared I would lose.

Chapter 22

The channels on Kang's flat-screen zoomed by at a speed that suggested he hadn't been paying much attention to the programing. He shut off the TV and placed the remote on the rustic wood-plank coffee table in front of him. Suzi was at the station preparing for the nightly newscast and normally didn't get home until after midnight. Kang always tried to catch the show so he could discuss it with her when she returned, but that night the case had his mind occupied.

Kang's phone chimed, and he opened an email from Kane. He looked at the photo she had sent him, and his initial reaction, without reading the email, was that it was the assassin girl, Sei. But because of the grain in the picture and the lighting, he could see Kane's hesitation. He took a few minutes to study Sei's outfit, but nothing about it struck him as having a purpose other than practicality.

After responding to Kane with his thoughts, he studied the pictures of the teapot once more. He had looked at them a dozen times and spent upward of two hours researching the drawings online with not much to show for his effort. *Why am I bothering with this?* He continued to ask himself that question over and over. It had overshadowed the other pertinent question: Where was the teapot?

Kang had sat in front of the computer again, ready to conduct more searches, when the obvious struck him.

Why don't I just ask the people at the tong?

Because you'll have to explain why you have pictures of that teapot.

I entered the premises legally and took pictures of various items. I was well within the law.

But you also took the pot.

They don't know that.

Kang looked at his watch. It was quarter to ten. *It's still early*, he told himself.

Twenty minutes later, Kang parked his Crown Vic outside the Hop Sing Tong. The shops on the street were closed except for the restaurant on the corner. Only a couple of tourists strolled down the lane. He could see no interior lighting through the windows of the tong, but the other tongs were dark as well.

Kang exited his vehicle and walked over to the entrance. Through the double glass doors, he could see that it was dark inside. Still, he knocked anyway. After multiple tries, he resorted to what he always knew he would do.

Looking behind him—the tourists were gone—Kang removed his lock-picking tools from the inner pocket of his jacket and went to work. After fifteen seconds, he had gained entrance to the tong.

130 *Coit Tower*

Once inside, Kang locked the door behind him, flicked on a small penlight, and cautiously made his way up the stairs. His destination was the top floor, as he was curious as to whether whoever had been previously sleeping there had been back. Had they noticed that the teapot was missing? Was that person there?

As he neared the top floor, Kang slowed his approach and softened his footsteps. The room was dark and quiet. But that didn't mean it was empty. Someone could be sleeping.

Kang stopped three steps short of the landing. The lone window was open, as it had been the last time. A bit of the moonlight seeped through, giving some transparency to the darkness. He directed his penlight over to the corner of the room where he remembered the bed to be. It was empty. He made a few more passes over the room with the light before he convinced himself that he was alone. Up the final steps he went.

As he walked toward the bed, he moved the tiny beam around the area. The white comforter was still on the bed, and the empty food packages were on the floor. Even the teacup seemed to be exactly where he remembered last seeing it. However, one thing stood out, something Kang wasn't expecting. Sitting next to the cup, as if it had never been removed, was the teapot he had taken.

Chapter 23

Kang took a sharp breath as he pulled his head back. A surge of prickles raced along his spine before shooting through both arms and tickling the tips of his fingers. He blinked in disbelief. Instinctively, he drew his gun and spun around, searching the room once more with his weapon and the penlight, the thumping in his chest unrelenting.

He looked. He listened. He moved quietly away from the bed, heading toward the bathroom on the far side of the room. The door was closed.

He and Kane had been watched that day when they entered the tong. He knew that much. How else could he explain the teapot making its way back home? More importantly, the question running through his head at the moment was whether someone was watching him then.

Kang worked to control his breathing, fearful it would disrupt the silence in the room. A heavy blanket of darkness still covered most of the room, and if it were an advantage, he intended to use it.

He proceeded as if he were not alone. Slow, purposeful steps brought him closer to the bathroom door. Once in arm's reach of the doorknob, Kang stood with his back against the wall to the left of the hinges. He knew the door opened outward from his previous search. If someone were hiding and armed inside there, he wouldn't be caught standing in the middle, in the fatal funnel.

Kang brought his weapon up to the middle of his torso. He reached across the door with his left hand and turned the knob softly. It was unlocked.

One. Two. Three.

He turned the handle quickly and pulled the door open. Kang stepped back away from the wall and peeked inside. The bathroom was empty.

Kang closed the door, moved over to the window, and looked outside. He checked his watch. It was a quarter to eleven. The street outside was quiet and empty. The restaurant on the corner had its lights on but appeared to be closed. He stuck his head out a bit farther. Below the window was the platform of the fire escape. Miss it, and that ten-foot drop turned into a fifty-foot splat on the sidewalk. Climbing down was doable, but there was no way back up from what he could see.

He holstered his weapon and walked over to the bed to inspect the teapot. He lifted the lid, and before he could peer inside, the aromatic scent of jasmine hit his nose. A finger check revealed a tiny bit of liquid at the bottom. It had been empty and dry when it was in his possession. Kang grabbed an empty paper bag near the bed and scooped up the teapot. Whoever had reclaimed it might have left some fingerprints.

He then hurried back down the stairs.

Once outside and sitting in the driver's seat of his car, he pulled out his cell phone and dialed Kane's number. "Abby, why I came to the tong isn't important right now... No, I'm not still inside; I'm sitting in my car. Listen... Listen, I found the teapot on the top floor, exactly where we first saw it... I'm not joking. But get this: Not only did someone take it from my car and return it to the tong, but that person drank tea from it. I'm having it dusted for prints... I know, I know. I completely agree. Whoever took the teapot from my car is probably the person you saw outside your window."

Chapter 24

Kang returned to Waverly Place the following day a little after eight in the morning. He wanted a conversation with the people in charge of the newly managed Hop Sing Tong, the ones who never seemed to be around, not even for their own grand reopening.

The tong still looked deserted, as it had the night before. No surprises there. The doors were locked the way he had left them, so Kang played along and knocked. He peered through the glass door but saw no one inside. *Fine, I'll wait.*

Kang crossed the street and bought a large coffee from the restaurant at the corner before settling back down in his vehicle. *I got all the time in the world.* He blew through the tiny opening of the coffee lid before taking a sip.

The residents of Chinatown had already started their day. He watched as the elderly puttered by. They seemed to be the only ones who got up early aside from the schoolchildren.

The men were usually on their way to meet friends at their daily hangout. A popular location on Waverly was the Blossom Bakery. There they would chat all day while drinking cheap green tea and munching on Chinese pastries. The women were simply getting an early start on their daily shopping needs, usually hitting up the fresh food markets that lined Stockton Avenue.

Kang sat quietly pressing the paper cup to his lips for a few minutes before pulling out his phone and texting Kane.

Kang: You up?

Abby: Yeah. What's up?

Kang: I'm camped outside the tong waiting for the owners to show up.

Abby: Sounds exciting. How long?

Kang: Couple of hours. I'll come back in the afternoon if needed.

Abby: Can your cigar-smoking friend help?

Kang: I'll call her later when the CCBA opens.

Abby: That day we searched the tong a curious man came up to my car.

Kang: What happened?

Abby: Reilly called before I could question him. He might know something.

Kang: What does he look like?

136 *Coit Tower*

Abby: Short. Wore a gray, ivy cap. Lots of sunspots on his face.

Kang: Did he have a white cane?

Abby: Yeah.

Kang: I think I see your guy.

An old fellow fitting that description had just appeared from a residential building across the street from the tong and started walking in the opposite direction. Kang exited the vehicle and hurried to catch up with him. He must have sensed Kang's approach, because the guy picked up his hobbling pace.

"Hold up. I want to talk to you. I'm Detective Kang with the San Francisco Police Department." Kang flashed his identification to the old man, who still seemed intent on getting away. Kang reached out and gently but firmly grabbed him by the arm. "Please. I just have a few questions. You're not in trouble."

The residents of Chinatown had been leery of the police ever since the first waves of immigrants had settled in the city. They tended to solve their own problems within their community. It was partly what had given the Triads their tight grasp on the neighborhood. They were often the ones residents turned to when a dispute needed to be settled.

The old man stopped tugging his arm away. "I not do anything wrong," he replied with an accent.

"I didn't say you did. You live there?" Kang pointed to the building.

The old man nodded.

"What's your name?"

"Liu Jie, but everyone call me Lester."

Kang nodded approvingly. "All right, Lester, tell me: you ever see people come and go from the Hop Sing Tong?"

"I don't know anything."

"That's not what I asked." Kang flashed a friendly smile. "Come on. Help me out."

The old man's eyes shifted from side to side before he looked up and down the street. "I see someone come at night, but not get good look. Very dark."

"Only at night? Never during the day?"

The old man nodded.

"What did this person look like?"

Lester shrugged.

"Old? Young? Did you see more than one person?"

"No, only one person. Not old like me. I only see once."

"Anything else you can tell me about this person? Is he associated with the tong?"

Lester placed both hands on his cane, leaning forward a bit and looking past Kang toward the direction of the tong.

"It's okay. No one is going to hurt you."

Lester stole a few more glances before raising his arm

138 *Coit Tower*

and pointing at the lone window at the top of the tong.

"Did you see someone in that window?"

Lester nodded. "Use window to go inside."

Chapter 25

Armed with the information from Lester, Kang didn't bother to call Ethel and headed straight over to the CCBA. He was officially questioning her. If she knew the people who had taken over the tong, she had information he wanted.

The office hours were nine to five. Kang arrived at half past nine. He had opted for the ten-minute walk rather than trying his luck with parking on Stockton.

Once inside, Kang saw Grace, who had just sat down behind her desk. She had what looked to be a fresh mug of coffee in her hand.

"Fancy seeing you here this early," she said. "Coffee?" She lifted her mug.

"I'm good. I had some earlier."

"You're in luck. She's normally not in the office this early. She even got here before me."

"Thanks." Kang smiled and delivered a knuckle knock on Grace's desk as he passed by. He hadn't heard Ethel's voice echoing in the short hall leading to her office. Unusual. Kang peered around the doorframe and leaned in. "Good morning."

Ethel jumped in her chair. "Dammit, Kyle, you almost gave me a heart attack."

"Sorry." Kang shrugged. He took a seat in front of her desk. "Why are you here so early?"

"I should ask you the same." Ethel closed the laptop she had open.

"I need to ask you a few questions."

"Uh oh," she said, peering over her reading glasses. "This sounds serious."

"It is. It's regarding a case I'm investigating."

Ethel leaned back in her chair and folded her hands across her lap. "How can I help?"

"The Hop Sing Tong, you know who took over, and I need to ask them a few questions. Where can I find them?"

"Why? What's happened?"

"Nothing's happened. I have a few questions, but nobody ever seems to be around when I stop by."

Ethel held up a finger while she picked up the receiver to the phone on her desk. She dialed, and after a few silent seconds of them staring at each other, she hung up. "No one's answering, but I'll make a few other calls. The person in charge there is Charles Yee. I've known him for a few years."

Kang's brow wrinkled. "Hmm, that name doesn't ring a bell." He removed a pen and a small notebook from his jacket and noted the name.

"He's a transplant from New York. Came out here

specifically to get the tong back in order." Ethel leaned forward. "May I ask about the case?"

"I'm working on a joint investigation with the FBI. We're chasing down a variety of angles. This is just one of them. Don't worry; he's not a suspect." Kang smiled, but the truth was, he hadn't ruled out the tong. After finding the missing teapot, it had him convinced that somehow the tong was still involved with the game. He just couldn't quite prove it yet.

Ethel nodded. "I'll get a hold of Charles for you. Don't worry."

Kang grasped both arms of the chair and pushed himself up. "Thanks, I appreciate it. The sooner the better." He moved around the desk and gave her a kiss on the cheek. "I owe you."

"Sunday brunch—the Palace," she called out as Kang exited her office.

Chapter 26

I hadn't been out of the house since the night Team Favela had attacked me, so I changed into running gear and headed downstairs. I walked out onto the front porch where Copeland was sitting.

"Where's your partner?" I asked as I sat next to him and put on my running shoes.

"He's in the back. Where are you heading?"

"For a run." I glanced up. "You're more than welcome to join me."

"I can't let you do that."

"You can't stop me. By the way, aren't you a bit bored sitting out here? Come on, go get changed." I had no idea if he had anything suitable for running. Both had ditched the suits after the first day and were content with jeans and hoodies.

"What if someone's waiting for you?"

"I'm a target sitting right here next to you just as much as I am on the road. I'm not going to hide." I lifted the hoodie I used for running just enough to show Copeland the shoulder holster housing my Glock.

"You've got three minutes." I stood up and started to

stretch. "If you're not back out here, you'll have to find me."

"Give me five." Copeland hurried inside.

I strapped my mini iPod onto my left arm and stuck my earbuds in my ears. I scrolled to the playlist titled "Rock the Road," hit play, and grinned as Ozzy screamed into my ears.

When Copeland returned, I gave him a few minutes to stretch, and then we hit the road. Boy, did it feel good.

Typical SF air: crisp, refreshing, and tingling in the nostrils. With the absence of clouds, the sun shone bright across the bay. I couldn't have asked for better conditions. We ran west on my street, Pfeiffer, then north on Columbus. I opted for a shorter route that morning, one that was just under three miles. It would take us along the Embarcadero past the famed Fisherman's Wharf and Pier 39 until Broadway and then back into North Beach—a good dose of flats and hills to get the blood flowing and the endorphins firing.

I didn't pay much attention to Copeland, only a few glances to see if he had kept up. He had his head on a permanent rotation of our surroundings. I saw Alcatraz as a gap between port buildings opened up and thought about the SF movie theme that my death should tie into. I wondered if studying the movies might give me any insight into recognizing a future attack. I made a mental note to have Reilly put a junior agent on the task of researching the movies.

The run, thus far, had helped me think through the problems I had been experiencing with the case. I thought about how I had been put on the defensive, having to guard myself from another attack. I wondered, if that hadn't been the case, would I be any further along?

It made me remember what my father used to say to me after a sparring session. "It's okay if you're backed up against the ropes, but don't stay there." That's what had happened to me. The mastermind had me leaning against them, and I hadn't done a damn thing about it. Ali was a master against the ropes, but I was no Ali. My style was closer to Sugar Ray—small, fast, and accurate with combos.

So why then had I been content to slug it out that way, a losing position for someone like me? I wasn't sure; maybe because the mastermind had proven to be an opponent I had never faced before. That reminded me of another thing my father had advised me to do: Adapt and come up with a different strategy. I knew I needed to go on the offensive. The mastermind assumed I would dig in and wait out the attacks, and so far, he had guessed right.

But which way forward? What offensive move should I take? I was a target, my attackers were essentially invisible, and I had no idea where or even who the mastermind was. How could I put an end to the game and not get myself killed at the same time?

A few minutes of heel against pavement, and the

answer came with complete clarity. *I'll make myself a bigger target.*

Chapter 27

Back at the house, I wasted no time putting my plan into place and put a call in to a trusted friend. "Everything is fine. I'll see you in a bit."

An hour later, I was freshly showered and had changed into jeans and a hoodie. The doorbell rang just as I had started to walk down the stairs. Standing outside on my porch with a smile on her face was my friend, Agent Tracy House.

"I'll have you know: I fought traffic all the way across the Bay Bridge."

I looked at my watch. "It's noon. What traffic are you talking about?"

"There was road work. You ready?"

"Yep." I gave my hoodie a courtesy pat out of habit to ensure I had my weapon before walking out the door.

Copeland watched all of this with a dumbfounded look. He must have thought he was invisible. He was. "Where are you heading?"

"I've got something in the car she needs to see firsthand," House called out as we walked down the driveway.

I didn't bother to look back. I wasn't sure if Copeland or House knew each other, but I was assuming she'd had to flash her badge to gain entrance to the porch. He knew she was friendly. I had counted on that. And it worked, because he sat back down in the wicker chair while House and I got into her vehicle and drove off. I wish I could have seen the look on his face.

It didn't take long for my phone to start ringing. "Abby, what are you doing?" Copeland asked.

"I needed to get outside. It'll help me think through the case."

"You were just outside."

"Yeah, I know, but I have more thinking I need to do. Don't worry; Agent House is with me. It's no different than if you were escorting me. We'll be back in a couple of hours."

"But my orders were—"

"I've got control of my mouth. Do you?"

After Copeland and I had come to an understanding, I hung up and tucked my phone into my hoodie's zippered pocket.

"What was that about?"

"One of the agents assigned to my security detail needed to cover his butt in the event that news of my little field trip makes it back to Reilly."

"Well, if everyone keeps their mouth shut…"

"I think he got the message."

I leaned back in my chair and stared out the window at the passing buildings. We were heading west on California Street toward Ocean Beach. A walk along the surf seemed like a good idea.

With traffic manageable, it only took twenty minutes before my toes were digging into the sand while salty sea spray filled my nose. House and I stayed just out of the grasp of the crashing surf that washed over the beach. The cawing and flapping of numerous seagulls encircled us during our walk.

I brought House up to speed on everything that had transpired since Park's death. She knew about the attack at my home but didn't know the details.

"Sheesh, Abby. Maybe Reilly is right. We're not talking about one guy stalking you."

"I get it, but sitting still and waiting to be attacked is exactly what the mastermind wants me to do. It effectively hampers my ability to investigate."

"You won't get any argument from me. It's actually a brilliant strategy in an effed-up sort of way. So, what's the plan? You're under your director's orders to stay put."

I dipped both hands into my jeans pockets. "I realize that, but it's time I helped Kang crack the connection between the Hop Sing Tong and the game."

"Well, if they are indeed connected, showing your face around Chinatown is one way to give this guy the middle finger. Is this what this little field trip is about? Because if it is, we shouldn't be here at the beach."

"Reilly wanted to set up a command post on my front lawn. I talked him out of it, but now I'm thinking that's exactly what needs to be done. We need to make this investigation as big and as public as possible."

"Won't that only draw more attention to you?"

"That's exactly what I want to happen. The mastermind has strength because we've kept quiet on the game and the killings that took place. It's time we let everyone know about Chasing Chinatown and what this person is doing."

A smile appeared on House's face. "I like it. Destroy his anonymity by going public. A press conference?"

"That and more. I'll give Reilly his command post— only it won't be outside my home."

An hour later, Copeland and Knox met House and me at the Hop Sing Tong. Knox started talking the second he exited their vehicle. "Abby, you can't just go running off. This is serious. We have a job to do, and—"

"I'm sorry," I said, putting a hand up. "It won't happen again. From this point forward, we're all joined at the hip."

Knox looked over at Copeland, who only shrugged. "What's going on here? Why did you ask us to meet you at the tong?"

"Because this," I said, pointing back at the building, "will be our new command post."

Chapter 28

It didn't take long for Knox, Copeland, and me to pack up a few personal items and rendezvous back at the tong. We were officially moving in, whether the owners liked it or not. House had already started the paperwork that would allow us to seize the property. We were making an asset grab, civil forfeiture. Under this law, the government could confiscate property without charging the owner so long as they believed that asset had been involved or associated with a crime. The tong would become the property of the U.S. government. Everything in it would be ours. Anything connected to the tong—cars, other offices, homes—would be seized. The building was the perfect location for our investigation and the beginning of the end for the mastermind and his sick game.

I had claimed the top floor of the tong. I wanted whoever came and went from that window to know they had a guest. I stripped the mattress of its bedding and fitted my own on it. I had a desk brought up from a lower floor and dry-erase boards attached to the walls.

I had just finished mapping out everything we knew to date about the game and the mastermind when Reilly appeared.

"Bold, Abby. Very bold."

"If we want to catch this bastard, we need to get back to what we do best."

"Seize assets?"

I chuckled. He walked over to the wall and looked at the information I had compiled. I had listed all the cities involved and their current status: defunct or in play. I also listed the names of the teams, the kills they had made, and whether they were apprehended, killed, or still at large. I even listed the names of anyone associated with the game or the investigation up on the wall—everyone from the mastermind to Sei to my friend Artie, the late detective in Bangkok. Every single action we were aware of had been noted. I wanted an eagle's-eye view of all that had taken place since day one of our investigation.

Reilly walked slowly along the timeline of events. He nodded every now and then but kept his thoughts to himself until he had reached the end of the wall. "Well, this certainly makes it easier to connect the dots."

"I agree."

"Fill me in on your next steps, Agent." He pulled up a chair and took a seat.

"I want to hold a news conference and reveal what we know about the game: how it's played, who the players are, the victims, the people in charge of running it..."

"Put it out in the open, have the media and the public

152   *Coit Tower*

help us put an end to this game."

"Exactly. By doing this, we can strip away the sheath of darkness that encompasses the game, the one thing I believe contributes to its power to exist."

"I like it," Reilly leaned back in his chair. "I think it'll work. But—"

"I know what you're about to say. It'll make me a bigger target. That's exactly what I want. I want to operate in the open because it will have the opposite effect. It'll make it harder to get at me. I expect the media to follow my every move. Waverly Place will be turned into a media encampment when I start telling my story."

"And once you've blown off the roof of this private party, then what?"

"This tong," I said, looking around. "It's the key to turning the corner on this investigation. Somehow, it's connected to the game." I filled Reilly in on the teapot and Kang's discovery of it back at the tong.

"So you two think whoever has been sneaking in and out of this place is also the person you saw in your tree?"

"Yes. In fact, I'll go one further. I think this mysterious person also killed Antonio Rocha."

"Team Favela?"

I nodded. "I believe that person sleeps in this bed, and I'm hoping for another run-in." From the look on Reilly's face, I couldn't tell if he had bought into my new approach to the investigation.

Ty Hutchinson 153

"I'll be honest, Abby: I'm on the fence. Shedding a light on the game, I think that's a smart move. But your next step forward is muddy at best."

I understood the pushback. I couldn't positively argue that relying on a connection of the tong with the game would lead to cracking the case, but that was how I investigated. I squeezed and squeezed until there was no place for them to run.

I let out a breath and shifted my weight from one foot to the other. "So, what are you saying?"

Before Reilly could answer, Kang appeared at the top of the stairs. "So it's true." He had a wide smile stretched across his face. "Having control of the tong will definitely help." Kang gave Reilly a courtesy nod as he walked over to the marker boards.

"Update me in two days," Reilly said as he stood. "I expect progress." He headed down the stairs.

With both hands resting on his hips, Kang turned to me. "What's he got to say about all this?"

"He's cautious, as usual, but he's given me enough rope to hang myself."

"Well, that's not what's going to happen. This is a brilliant move."

"Your praise... it's so... unlike you." I grinned.

"I'm serious." Kang grabbed a marker and wrote the name "Charles Yee" off to the side of where I had written "mastermind"; I had him positioned at the very top of pyramid of people involved in the game.

"Who's that?" I asked.

"He's in charge of the tong, but funny enough, he's never around." Kang briefed me on the conversation he'd had with Ethel that morning.

"How well does she know this guy?"

"Well enough, I suppose." Kang pocketed his hands into his slacks. "But she's coming up empty on making an introduction. Finding him should be our next step. The fact that he's made himself unavailable only makes me believe that he and this tong are involved. I've already reached out the NYPD's 5th Precinct. They cover Chinatown. Ethel said he was a community leader there."

"This guy sounds guiltier by the second." I moved toward my laptop and logged into the NCIC server. After a few minutes, I looked back at Kang. "It appears the bureau doesn't officially have anything on the guy, but that doesn't mean we haven't heard of him. I'll put a call in to the New York office and see if his name yields anything useful." *Could this guy be our elusive mastermind?*

I walked back over to the board where Kang had written his name and drew a question mark next to the mastermind. "If your friend Ethel knows this guy so well, well enough she can pick up a phone and reach him, surely she must have a picture of him. But what has my brain spinning is if this guy really is the mastermind, what's Ethel doing hanging out with him?"

"Yeah, you're right. But she might not know. To start with, we can canvas Chinatown, and if he's here, we can force him out of hiding."

I looked at my watch. It was nearing four thirty in the afternoon. "Let's pay Ethel another visit, see what sort of progress a day has allowed her to make."

Chapter 29

Copeland and Knox met us on our way down the stairs. "What are our next steps?" Knox asked.

"We're heading over to Stockton. There's someone there we need to question. You two should join us. The more the merrier."

"We'll bring the car around."

"Let's walk. It'll give us another opportunity to address the media."

No sooner had the four of us exited the building than we were ambushed by the hordes of reporters camped outside. It was exactly what I had wanted to happen. I held up a hand to quiet them as we walked. "The investigation is still ongoing, but we are making significant progress."

"Can you tell us anything more about the connection of the tong with the game?" one of the reporters asked.

"We do have new information," I said, pausing. "We could use the public's help in locating a Mr. Charles Yee, the person responsible for managing the tong."

"Is he the man behind the game, the so-called mastermind?"

"I can neither confirm nor deny that, but the sooner we

can locate him, the better we will be able to answer that question."

"The SFPD is working on securing a positive ID on this guy," Kang added. "We'll circulate a picture once we do."

With a swarm of reporters following us, we had a ten-foot buffer zone separating me from any opportunistic player of the game. The media, in their quest for information, provided a layer of fat—the good kind. I wouldn't go so far as to call it a secured zone, but still, it helped.

I leaned in closer to Kang. "Well, we've just outed Mr. Yee. If he's completely innocent, this should bring him to our attention."

"I'd say we did more than that. We just pegged him as the mastermind."

"We didn't. The media did," I said with a smile.

"Agent Kane," came another voice from the throng. "Where are you heading now?"

"The CCBA on Stockton."

"What can you tell us about their involvement with the game?"

"I wouldn't go so far as to say they're involved, but they might possess information that can lead us to Mr. Yee."

The media hub walked in step with us all the way to the front steps of the CCBA, and we did nothing but welcome

158 *Coit Tower*

them to wait for our return, affording us the same security buffer on our walk back to the tong.

Once inside, Knox and Copeland took positions near the entrance while Kang led me back to Ethel's office. I could hear her voice booming from a room at the end of the hallway.

As soon as we rounded the corner, she stopped talking and covered the phone with her palm. "Kyle, what are you doing here?"

"I'm sorry to bother you twice in one day."

I stepped out from behind Kang, prompting Ethel to politely end the call.

"Agent Kane, I didn't see you. Please sit." She motioned to the two chairs in front of her desk.

"We have more questions," I said.

Ethel's eyes focused on Kang. "I know why you're here. It's been all over the news. I've been trying to track down Charles ever since our meeting this morning. I don't understand it. He's always returned my calls right away. I'm beginning to worry."

"Ethel," I said, "do you have a picture of him?"

"If he's in some sort of trouble, we can use the public's help in finding him," Kang added.

"Oh, I'm sure I do." Ethel reached down, lifted her purse onto her lap, and dug around until she found her smartphone. She adjusted her glasses as she used one hand to maneuver through the screens on the phone. "Hmmm, maybe I'm wrong. I thought for sure I had one." She looked up over her glasses. "I've been to a couple of group luncheons with Charles, and we always take pictures at these events, but it doesn't look like I have any. Strange." She clucked her tongue. "I'll dig around and ask a few friends we have in common and see if I can locate a picture for you."

"Kyle mentioned that Mr. Yee was a community organizer back in New York."

"Yes, his most notable work was for the On Leong Tong."

"Does the tong have a website? Maybe his picture is—" Before I could finish my sentence, Kang had his phone out, Googling the tong.

"I got nothing coming up for On Leong," he reported. "I've heard of them but don't know much about their organization."

"They might not have a website—typical for most tongs," Ethel said. "I'm trying to change that. Anyway, they're located on Mott Street in New York's Chinatown district. They also go by the name Chinese Merchants Association. Try that."

Kang found a simplistic website that gave out information on the association along with upcoming events and activities. "No pictures, and I don't see any mention of Charles Yee."

"Doesn't surprise me," Ethel said. "He wasn't a

member. He only consulted."

"For a guy who's done so much, he's certainly hard to pin down," Kang said as he closed the browser on his phone. "Is there anybody there that can help us locate him?"

"I'm one step ahead of you." Ethel waved a finger. "I've already put in a call. It's been a while since he's done any work with them, but I'm hopeful."

"What kind of work did he do for them exactly?" I asked.

"Well, during the early eighties up until the early nineties, the tong had been under the control of the Ghost Shadows, a Chinese gang. Charles had been instrumental in helping the authorities nab their leader, Wing Yeung Chan, and ultimately wrestled control of the tong away from the gang and back into the hands of the Chinatown community."

"That case rings a bell," Kang said. "I think Chan was indicted on murder and racketeering charges."

"That sounds about right." Ethel nodded. "Charles' experience with that is partly the reason why I thought he would make a good fit here. We—well, Chinatown, really—wanted to ensure that the Hop Sing Tong didn't fall back into its old ways."

"Partly? What was the other reason?" I asked.

"His wife died a few years ago. They had no children. In one of my visits to New York, he mentioned that he was looking for a change, something that would take him out of the Big Apple. I've always kept that in the back of my mind."

"So it was your decision to hire him?" I asked.

"The decision was made by various community business owners in Chinatown. All I did was bring Charles to their attention." Ethel let out a soft breath as she looked away.

"Were you two close?" I questioned.

"Not originally. The distance kept our relationship mostly businesslike. But with his arrival out here, we got to know each other a bit better. I considered him a friend. There is no way he is involved with anything illegal."

"We didn't say he was. Is there a reason why you thought of that?"

Ethel shifted in her chair. "Look, I won't play dumb. I know why you're asking about him. I've seen some of the interviews you've given to the media. The FBI is claiming that the tong is connected to this Chasing Chinatown game, if there is one."

"What makes you think there isn't?"

"I'm not discounting that people were killed and that the tong had been under control of the Triads, but I find it hard to believe that it's still involved. Jing Woo and his gang were decimated by the FBI."

"Well, someone else got to Jing before we did," I said.

"Charles is not this so-called mastermind, if that's what you're thinking. Believe me."

"And what makes you so sure of that?"

"He... he can't be. He's such a nice man. Not a mean bone in his body." Ethel clasped her hands together and placed them in her lap. Her head lowered, her eyes softened, and her shoulders slumped—a sudden realization, I imagined.

"I had such high hopes. I thought we were finally putting an end to the organized crime that has plagued our community here in San Francisco from the beginning." Ethel looked up at us. "Could I have been so wrong about him?"

"We need to find him, Ethel," Kang said. His voice had taken a serious turn. "Innocent or not, he's gone missing, and in my experience, that's never a good sign."

Chapter 30

We waited until we were back inside the tong before discussing our conversation with Knox and Copeland. While we needed attention from the media, I had been mindful of the information fed to them. They were merely pawns.

We gathered on the top floor, away from prying ears and microphones.

"So this Yee guy, you think she's trying to protect him, or is she being genuine?" Knox said what everyone had been thinking.

"Kyle knows her better than I do." I turned toward him. "What's your take?"

"No way." Kang shook his head. "I've known Ethel for a long time. I don't believe she would keep anything from me, especially something like this."

"Still, it's a little suspect that she claims to be his friend and has known him for years, yet can't produce a picture or get him on the phone." I shrugged. "Just saying."

"I know how it looks, but I'm willing to give her the benefit of the doubt. I wouldn't wait on her to produce this guy, though. I've got his phone number now and I'll be calling nonstop."

"Not having an ID on this guy isn't making things easier," Copeland added as he walked over to the window and looked down below. "Let's hope that, with the media blasting his name out there, we're able pick up a lead on his whereabouts."

"Another mystery guy to add to the list," Knox said with breathy sarcasm.

I couldn't blame him. An elusive mastermind, a ghost assassin, and a faceless community organizer made up our cast of top suspects.

"There's Lester," Kang offered.

"Who?" I asked.

"The old man you bumped into outside of the tong." Kang grabbed a dry-erase marker and wrote his name on the board. "I questioned him earlier this morning. He said he saw someone enter this room through that window at night, so no specifics on what the person looked like."

"Using the window as a door only confirms our suspicions that something sketchy is happening in this tong," I said.

"Lester couldn't give a description? No specifics?"

Kang shook his head. "I think the guy has cataracts. We're lucky he even witnessed it. Still, since we have everyone else on the board, might as well add him."

"Cataracts? Sheesh, two steps forward, three back," Knox commented before heading for the stairs. "I think that pot of coffee should be done brewing."

We all followed him down to the second floor. Kang picked up the TV remote and turned on the large flat-screen TV. Chasing Chinatown dominated every news station. "The first part of our plan is hitting on all cylinders."

We watched for a few minutes before Copeland broke the silence. "Man, we need to convert this attention into action. It's rare that a case gets so much attention. I mean, CNN is covering this story nonstop."

"I agree," Kang chimed in.

"Let's give it time, see what information comes back. In the meantime, I'll continue giving interviews to feed the frenzy."

Knox reappeared from the kitchen with a pot of coffee in one hand and a bunch of paper cups in the other. He set the brew down on the table. "Abby, I've got a kettle of hot water on the stove for you."

"Thanks." I headed into the kitchen, where I had left my tin of loose-leaf tea. I drink only *Tieguanyin*. I pried the cover off, grabbed a pinch, and dropped the leaves into an empty mug. I poured water from the kettle, and within seconds, the water began to take on that familiar green hue. I took a tiny sip. *Another minute and it'll be perfect.* I placed a napkin over the cup and headed toward the stairs. "I'll be up on the fifth if anybody needs me."

Chapter 31

Zoric, Petrovic, and Adrijana settled in at the Holiday Inn on Van Ness Avenue shortly after seven p.m. Empty takeout boxes from the diner next door littered the top of a small table near the sliding door leading out to a narrow balcony. A twelve-pack of Budweiser sat on the elongated desktop that ran the length of one side of the room under a window of the same dimensions. The air conditioning unit was a floor model, and its hum was nothing less than industrial.

"This is bullshit, man," Petrovic blurted after taking a swig from his beer bottle. He sat slouched in a chair, which was tucked away in the corner of the room, with one booted foot on the carpeted floor and the other resting on an ottoman. They couldn't afford two rooms, and all the rooms with two twin beds were occupied. They had settled for one with a king-sized bed and had requested a rollaway bed. Guess who got the rollaway. "Why don't we just go to a cheaper hotel so we can get two rooms?"

"This is a cheap hotel," Adrijana countered, her tone laced with disgust, as usual. She and Zoric were sitting on the bed, resting back against the pillows that lined the headboard.

"I'm sure there are cheaper hotels," Petrovic continued.

Adrijana looked at Zoric. "I'm not staying in some rat-infested, piece-of-shit place."

"Oh, look who's too good." Petrovic chugged more of his beer.

Zoric hated being around both of them at the same time. The two bickered nonstop, with him always forced to side with one or the other. He worried that bringing Adrijana with them would hamper their ability to complete the Attraction. But in addition to bankrolling the trip, Adrijana had also secured counterfeit passports for each of them. Zoric and Petrovic had had no choice but to bring her along.

"The sooner we get rid of this FBI agent, the sooner we can collect our money," Zoric said. "We must act fast." They had no idea how many other teams had come to finish the game. Updates were no longer being supported on the application.

"We have no weapons. How are we supposed to grab her?" Petrovic asked. "I can choke that bitch, but it's not like she's waiting outside for me."

"We need a plan," Adrijana noted. "Plus, we can't submit just any picture of her dead. It has to tie into the theme."

"I told you guys, *The Rock*. If we use that movie, we will win."

168   *Coit Tower*

"And what is the *plan*?" Adrijana rolled her eyes. "You going to blow her up in a building with all the C-4 explosive you have in your back pocket? No, wait. You want to lock her up in a cell inside Alcatraz?"

"Drago, I can't take this shit. This bitch is pissing me off."

"Who are you calling a bitch?"

"Shut up! Shut up!" Zoric had tried to stay out of it. He'd worked hard to ignore most of their conversation, focusing on the MMA match on the television. He turned his head to his friend. "I like that movie too, but she's got a point. We need something that is easy and fast." Zoric flipped through the channels and quickly found a news station broadcasting the Chasing Chinatown investigation. "Look at this. Everybody already knows about the game."

"So what?" Petrovic sneered.

"So what? How do you expect us to get anywhere near her?" Zoric threw both of his hands into the air. "Right now this woman is surrounded by reporters and FBI agents." He grabbed his beer off the bedside table. "The more she talks, the harder it is for us."

They had lost the element of surprise, and it pissed off Zoric. Sure, Kane didn't know their identities, but that botched attempt by the sniper, the attack on her at her home, and the FBI's full disclosure of the game were making it damn near impossible to get anywhere near her, even with her out in the open.

Petrovic chugged the rest of his beer before opening another bottle and draining half of it in one gulp. Zoric knew silence was Petrovic's way of acknowledging that what he had said was right. He then looked over at Adrijana and thought about all the money she had spent. The emptiness in her eyes told him she wished she hadn't. Zoric turned his attention back to the TV while his mind wrestled to find a solution to their predicament.

Silence fell over the room.

Adrijana avoided looking at the men as she sipped from the bottle of red wine she held captive between her thighs. Even with her limited knowledge of criminal activities, she knew Zoric and Petrovic didn't have the equipment needed to make a full frontal assault, not with the security detail in place and the constant media coverage surrounding Agent Kane. To win, they would need to break from their comfort zone and do what no other team had attempted.

She swirled the wine in her mouth before breaking the silence. "What if we used her partner, the cop? You know, as bait."

Chapter 32

The tong had all the comforts needed for us to live there. Whatever it lacked, we brought in. We requisitioned extra cots for Knox and Copeland on the fourth floor and a few other agents on the third. There was a kitchen on the second floor, and the third and fourth each had a bathroom with a shower. The top floor, which I had commandeered, lacked a shower, but I did have a toilet and a basin. It would suffice. In all, a total of six agents, including me, would be staying at the tong while a handful of support staff showed up daily.

Knox reinforced the crappy lock on the front door as well as the locks on all the lower-level windows that opened onto the fire escape. Two security cameras were installed outside the front of the tong. Knox and his team took turns monitoring the video feeds.

Kang convinced his supervisor to add foot patrols in Chinatown during the day and to increase vehicle patrols at night. Also, in an agreement struck by all parties, traffic on Waverly Place had been temporarily halted by the SFPD specifically so the news vans could camp outside—a much-needed pipeline of info to the public and the first welcomed media circus I could ever recall.

Up to that point, every aspect of my plan had been successfully executed—a nice relief considering the difficulty of the investigation. Back in the beginning, when we were chasing Team Carlson, we'd had no idea what capturing a couple of lunatics would unveil.

I stood still, staring at the boards on the wall, when I heard someone clear their throat. I turned around and found Kang standing at the top of the stairs. "You ready for your first night in the tong?" he asked, walking toward me with both hands in his pants pockets.

"Sure. The bed's a little stiff, but it'll do. I'm sure we can scrounge up another cot if you're interested in joining our sleepover."

He smiled. "I would, but Suzi's expecting me."

I sat and motioned for him to take a seat in one of the chairs I had brought up from the rec room on the second floor. "How's that going?"

His head bobbed from side to side. "We've had better days."

Oh, you must be referring to the time you were with me in Bangkok. I bit my tongue and only looked at him.

He had lowered his head a little, and his eyes drifted down toward the floor. "I thought things would be different since she came back from Florida, you know?" He looked back at me. "But they're not."

You know the saying: fool me once... Forget it. I'll

listen because you're my friend. I remained silent.

"There are times when we're happy, and then there are times when we're not. I try to think that these up and down moments are simply part of relationships, but I know Suzi and I just have a lot of differences."

His eyes had drifted back to the floor, and we both remained quiet for a few moments before he spoke again.

But this time, he sat up and clasped his hands together. "I'm sorry for laying my girlfriend problems on you." A half smile appeared.

"Hey, that's what friends are for." I'd be lying if I said I wasn't cheering inside at the thought of Kang dumping her prima donna butt, but I didn't like seeing my usually upbeat partner wallowing in sadness. Kang was a nice guy with a good heart. He deserved someone who could appreciate what he had to offer. *Someone like me. Wait, what? Focus, Abby. Stop it with the superhero crush.*

As far as I could tell in listening to him talk about Suzi, she sounded like a major attention whore who treated him like an afterthought. I mean, she must be dynamite in the sack, because she comes off as a raging bitch everywhere else. The few times I was forced to see them interact, she would constantly talk over him and correct him over the minutest details. I swear, I must have mentally punched her face a million times while laughing hysterically. Kang could do much better. "Anytime you want to talk, I'm here for you."

His smile grew. "Thanks. I really appreciate it." A moment later, he stood. "Well, it's getting late. I'll see you first thing in the morning."

As I watched him walk back down the stairs, I thought about that day in Chinatown when we had first met. "What a dork" was my first impression. *Yeah, so I was wrong about the guy.*

Later that night, I stood near the open double-casement window in my room, lost in a myriad of thoughts: the case, my family, my partner—more than enough to keep me up much longer than they already had.

I let out a small yawn and reached out to close the window but stopped myself. Even though the night air was chilly and filled with enough drifting fog to obscure the view of the building across the lane, I wondered about the room's other occupant.

I left the window open and snuggled under the covers of my bed. I fell asleep with one last thought swimming in my head: Would the person I saw in my tree visit me? Again?

I hoped so.

Chapter 33

Adrijana's idea gained traction immediately. Zoric wrote the detective's name down, thanks to the media, and Adrijana was able to Google his address successfully.

To figure out what they were up against and if there were something about Detective Kang that they could take advantage of, Zoric wanted to start surveillance right away. What type of residence did he live in? Did he live alone? This was Petrovic's responsibility. In the meantime, Zoric and Adrijana would hit up a nearby army surplus store for some much-needed equipment.

Forty minutes later, Petrovic exited the cab at the intersection of Hyde and Jackson, about a block north of the detective's home address. He approached the address from across the street.

Foot traffic at that time of night was minimal. There were a few people visiting the convenience store. A man walking his Chihuahua passed by, but he seemed too involved with his phone conversation to pay any attention to the other people on the street. Petrovic also noticed rail tracks running down the middle of Hyde Street but hadn't seen any passing cable cars.

Ty Hutchinson 175

When he reached the address, he found himself staring at a fairly average-looking Victorian duplex. It looked nothing like the fancy houses he saw farther up the street. According to the information Adrijana had fed him, Detective Kang lived at 1603-A—the door on the left with its lights off. He assumed the detective was still in Chinatown.

To the left of the building was a concrete pad big enough to park a car. Toward the back was a wooden gate about eight feet high. Pressed up against the right side of the building was a carriage house. Either the neighbors weren't home or they were fast asleep.

Petrovic crossed over to inspect the driveway. He noticed oil stains on the white concrete where the detective parked his car and that the wooden gate was actually made up of two separate gates.

Petrovic slipped around the first gate and passed two trash containers before cornering around the second. It led him to a small, shared backyard behind the building.

Petrovic checked the back door of unit A and found it locked—not a major obstacle. He peered into the window just to the right of the door and saw a small laundry room. The window glass was thin against his knuckles when he rapped. His assessment thus far was that the building was accessible. The only question he hadn't an answer for was whether the home had an alarm system. Petrovic had noticed a few homes with stickers in the windows touting

Brinks Home Security.

Satisfied with what he saw, Petrovic backtracked to the sidewalk out front and walked over to the convenience store, where he bought a pack of cigarettes. He lit one and took a seat at the bus stop near the intersection. From there he could keep an eye on the Victorian and not look out of place.

No sooner had he sat than a car slowed and turned into the driveway next to the Victorian. Petrovic perked up as he watched a lanky Asian man in a dark suit exit the vehicle. *Detective Kang.* He watched him walk behind the gate with a bag in his hand and, soon after, he reappeared without it before heading toward the front door. A light lit up the front parlor window on the first floor, and Petrovic saw the detective pass by. After that, he didn't see him again.

Petrovic texted Zoric what he had discovered so far and told him he wanted to watch the home for a bit longer. Zoric replied that he and Adrijana had picked up some useful supplies.

It was a little past midnight when Petrovic decided to call it a night. There was nothing more to see. But just as he stood, a news van for KTVU stopped outside the Victorian. A tall, thin Asian woman exited the vehicle. As she hurried up the stairs toward the door leading into 1603-A, Petrovic heard the driver call out, "I'll pick you up tomorrow morning at nine."

The van caught the light at the intersection and came to

a stop. The street was deserted. The convenience store stood dark and empty. Petrovic sprang into action.

A white male with a bushy beard sat in the driver's seat with the window rolled down. On-ear headphones hugged his head as he nodded rhythmically to a beat. The driver didn't hear Petrovic's approach. He never even looked his way, but the loud smack of bone against bone sounded like a gunshot to Petrovic in the quiet neighborhood.

Within seconds, Petrovic was in the driver's seat of the van, and lying across the passenger seat was the unconscious driver. Petrovic drove up the street to an area where the trees lining the sidewalk were dense, blocking out the streetlights. He parked the vehicle and moved the man to the rear of the van, where there was an array of electronic cables scattered. He picked one, wrapped it around the man's neck, and pulled tight—holding it much longer than he really needed.

It took Petrovic twenty minutes to find a dumpster where he could dispose of the body. On the way back to the hotel, he texted Zoric. "Good news. I have a new plan."

Chapter 34

"You idiot!" Adrijana's voice ricocheted off the walls of the underground parking garage.

Zoric grabbed her arm. "Keep your voice down."

"What the hell kind of plan is this?" she continued with a hushed tone through gritted teeth.

The three of them stood next to the news van that Petrovic had driven back to the hotel. He had already fed them the details of how he'd ended up with it.

"This is a great idea, but you're too stupid to know any better," Petrovic sneered.

"Stupid?" Adrijana's forehead crinkled as she pulled her head back into her neck. "We're not here for one day, and you've killed someone and stolen their van. And not just any van—a news van. How soon before someone knows it's missing?"

"I told you, we have until nine o'clock tomorrow morning. That's when he said he would pick up the girl."

"Adrijana, I know things are moving fast, but this is a good plan," Zoric said. "Posing as a news team will give us access to the agent."

She couldn't deny that. For the most part, she largely

stayed out of Zoric and Petrovic's criminal escapades and therefore didn't see firsthand what they actually did for a living. "What do we know about being a news team?"

"What's to know? I'll be the producer, Branko will be the cameraman, and you, my beautiful one," Zoric said, cupping the side of her face gently, "you will be the reporter."

"I don't know how to interview."

"You don't have to. We just need to get access to her, someplace where we can be alone. That's when we'll kill her."

"And we're supposed to just walk away?" Adrijana's line of questioning continued.

"Yeah," Zoric smiled as he turned to Petrovic and slapped him on the back. The two men obviously thought the plan was foolproof. Being that Petrovic had pretty much committed them by killing the driver and stealing his van, she had no other choice but to go along.

As the three of them walked back to the elevator, Zoric slipped an arm around Adrijana. "Tonight you watch the news, write down a few questions, see how a reporter acts. You'll be fine."

"You said I wouldn't have to interview her."

"It's just in case."

They exited the elevator, and a short walk down the hall put them back into their room. Petrovic went for the corner, picking up a beer from the fridge along the way, and plopped down in the chair. Zoric turned on the TV and made himself comfortable on the bed. Adrijana lay next to him against the headboard. "Okay, say we get her alone and kill her. How do we satisfy the game?"

"Ah, I already know the perfect movie: the last Dirty Harry film." He looked at her. A smile formed. "It's about celebrity killings. In the movie, Dirty Harry is one of the people on the list. In our version, it's Dirty Kane."

Chapter 35

I squinted as I peered at the time on my phone: three a.m.

No one had shaken me awake or called out my name. A loud disturbance outside hadn't alerted my ears. The cool air that flooded the room hadn't been the culprit. As far as I could recall, I had simply opened my eyes.

I turned onto my side to place my phone back on the small nightstand only to realize my holstered weapon, the one I had left on the nightstand before turning in, had gone missing.

I drew a sharp breath as a flurry of thoughts exploded in my head. Before I could make sense of any of them, a voice—a familiar one—interrupted my thought process. "Knock, knock. Who's there?"

My eyes darted to the area from which the voice had emanated. My breathing halted instinctively, and adrenaline-fueled blood tore throughout my body, shaking off any remaining remnants of sleep.

I held my phone up, and the white glow from the screen penetrated the dark. My eyelids flapped open and shut as I sought the person behind the voice. I didn't have to search for very long before a figure appeared from the depths of the darkness.

Sei!

She looked exactly as I remembered her, except now she wore a black jumpsuit that fit her physique like a glove. It appeared to be the same one that she had worn in the surveillance footage Park had given me. *I guess she was responsible for that kill.*

"I expected a much more enthusiastic response," she said dryly.

"Sorry to disappoint." The room fell dark again as the light from my phone shut off. I hit the menu button again, reinvigorating it. She had moved a bit closer in that span of time. The light popped against her porcelain skin while her hair blended into the darkness behind her. She wore heavy eyeliner, making her gaze darker. Deadlier. Her plump, pink lips were devoid of the hot-red lipstick she had worn in Bangkok.

"Must you keep that annoying light on?"

"I happen to like it."

"Suit yourself." She grabbed one of the chairs and positioned it ten feet from the bed and took a seat. "It's a crime that I infiltrated your"—she looked around the room—"defenses."

"Don't flatter yourself. I purposely left the window open." I sat up and slid my legs toward the side of the bed so I could better look at Sei—and to better position myself to react. Even though we were seemingly having a cordial conversation, I knew firsthand how dangerous she could be. The worst thing I could do was lower my guard. I tilted the light down for a better look around the nightstand.

"Fear not. Your gun is in a safe place."

Bathroom? Cabinet? Outside on the fire escape?

"Are you scared? Don't be. If I had wanted to kill you, I could have easily about a million times by now."

"Well, then, if you're not here to kill me, why did you show up?"

Sei stood without answering me and took another look around the room, mainly the area around the nightstand.

"I don't see my teapot anywhere. I will be needing that back."

"Fear not. Your teapot is in a safe place," I said, mimicking her. Kang had taken the pot during his second visit to the tong to see if he could grab prints off it. It had come up empty.

"It would be in your best interest to return it to me."

"You managed to find it on your own the first time we took it."

Sei didn't respond. I watched her casually stroll over to the window as if my presence posed no threat. I could see a seven-inch blade strapped to the outside of her left hip. *That's it? Just a knife?* She also wore some sort of utility belt that had three small pouches positioned around her lower back. *More weapons?* A small black backpack held what I guessed was the rest of her assassin equipment.

She placed her right foot on the windowsill and gracefully lifted herself up into a crouched position with no noticeable effort. I shimmied forward on the bed until the balls of my bare feet touched the linoleum floor.

"Moving off that bed would be a grave mistake," she said, her voice low and steady.

I held my position even though it was clear that she was about to bolt from the building. "You didn't answer my question."

"Hmmph. Yes, your question. I came here to warn you." She placed her hands on either side of the window frame and repositioned her body so that she faced outward.

"Warn me about what?" I straightened up, eager for her answer.

She looked back at me. Her eyes disappeared as she tilted her head down slightly. Our stare down seemed to go on for an eternity. And then she leaped, disappearing into the gray—but not before uttering six words that punched me directly in the chest.

"Your children are in danger. Hurry."

Chapter 36

After landing on the fire escape directly below the window, Sei maneuvered across a thin railing before leaping over to the fire escape of the adjacent building. From there, she slithered up a metal drainage pipe and pulled herself onto the roof, all in a matter of seconds. Thanks to the heavy fog blanketing the city that night, she knew Agent Kane would have lost sight of her at that point.

She hurried across the flat rooftop, executing a dance of one-handed vaults over a maze of air ducts until she reached the edge of the roof and the end of the block. From there, she performed a series of two-handed drops along a couple of window ledges before shinnying across a horizontal pipe and finally dropping down into a small alley. She darted across Clay Street and into another alley. Hugging the brick wall, she moved through the quiet night until she reached a small metal doorway. A knocking sound followed by a squeak signaled that she had opened the door and entered the building.

She stared down a dark, narrow hallway with a low ceiling. The cool air was damp and clung to her as she moved forward. Her footsteps were light and quick along the cement flooring, masking her presence. She slowed her advance and listened. Yet even with silence in her favor, a figure stepped into the hallway near the end and knowingly waited for her approach.

The figure spoke first. "Is it done?"

"Yes," Sei replied. "Still, I don't know why you asked me to do that. None of the players are aware of the family's location." Sei had gotten lucky that night at Kane's house. She had overheard one of the agents mention the name of the B&B during a phone conversation. A few days later, she had ID'd Kane's children and her mother-in-law at the location.

"I am not paying you to question my orders, only to execute them."

Sei said nothing more.

"The teams. What news do you have for me?"

"There are only two active teams in town: Team Kitty Kat and Team Balkan. However, neither has attempted a move on the agent."

"What about the other teams?"

"Unless they show up in the city, I can't know if they have plans to continue with the game. I cannot be everywhere at the same time."

The mastermind had disabled most of the app's functions with the change in the game dynamics to prevent the FBI from further using the game for its investigation.

Until that point, the mastermind had allowed Kane to

continue to access Chasing Chinatown out of sheer entertainment. It was added joy to see how things would play out with little fear that it would become a liability to the game. But with the change in the gameplay, it could pose problems. Unfortunately, disabling most of the app prevented the mastermind from tracking each team, short of messaging them for information. Sei's job was to keep an eye on them. She was to do what the app had done so well and more.

"I think it's safe to say the other teams have forfeited," Sei said.

"What makes you say that?" the figure asked.

"It's winner take all. Timing is now an element to consider. If the other teams were serious contenders, they would already be here."

"What's taking the two teams so long to strike?"

"Probably her relocation to the tong. There's only one entrance into that building. I know what you're thinking, and those teams are not me. Secondly, there are five other agents living there with her, not to mention the others that show up during the day. Thirdly, the media encampment outside the building. Fourth, the increased SFPD foot patrols in Chinatown. Shall I continue?"

"Your sarcasm has not gone undetected. I suggest you seriously work on controlling it."

Sei shifted her weight back to one leg. "Don't think for one second that I am afraid of you."

"And don't you think for one second that I cannot have you killed, even with all of the skills *I* have helped you to acquire."

A few moments of tense silence followed as the two stared at each other in the dark. Sei knew she could easily dispose of the mastermind, but that wasn't what gave her pause. The repercussions that would follow captured that honor. She might be able to escape the city. She might be able to hide, but the inevitable would happen. The mastermind's network of trusted mercenaries would come after her. And they wouldn't stop, either, not until she was dead. A life spent looking over her shoulder wasn't something she coveted.

She swallowed her pride. "I think both teams are capable of figuring out a way to get to the agent," Sei said. "It's only a matter of time."

"What assurances can you give me?"

"I can give no such thing," Sei said, letting out a dismissive breath. Sei really had no interest in the outcome. She only cared about doing her job and collecting the remaining half of her fee.

After dismissing Sei, the mastermind remained behind. Kane had made a move on the chessboard that the mastermind had not seen ahead of time, and it had proved to be problematic. However, there was one other play that could be made, one that could counter Kane's latest antics—one that had already been decided on.

The mastermind had a number of mercenaries who were extremely loyal beyond the money. At any moment, the mastermind could tap in to those killing machines. While Sei had been contracted to help with the operations of the game, the mastermind had put another assassin in place in the event things went south—an insurance policy.

The mastermind had spent years developing the game. It brought pride, it brought joy, but most of all, it brought endless entertainment. But what the mastermind had never figured on encountering was a person like Abby Kane. *How could someone single-handedly cause so much disruption?* The game was supposed to be unbreakable and unstoppable. And yet the mastermind was about to do the unthinkable: discontinue the game. Because of her.

The smartphone cast a white glow as the mastermind opened the Chasing Chinatown application. The animated dragon in the intro brought forth a smile, even though a final winner would never emerge. Returning to normal gameplay had been out of the question.

The mastermind had considered going out with a bang, orchestrating some sort of fantastic killing brouhaha, but after much consideration, it simply wouldn't suffice. No, there was really only one way to even the score. Kane had killed the mastermind's baby. It was time to return the favor.

Mastermind: Terminate the children.
Agent Lin: Roger that.

Chapter 37

A surge of emptiness filled my belly as I took a step back from the window. Sei's last words played on a loop, causing my legs to give way. I collapsed onto my knees. My hand released its grip on the window frame and flopped to my side. Tears bubbled and crested, streaking my face. I gasped louder with each breath as my chest tightened. I was the target, not my children. They should be coming after me. Only me. *Keep it together, Abby.*

I tried. I really did.

But the reality of the situation had wrapped its arms around me and begun to squeeze. Guilt scrutinized my decision making. Fear battered my will. Images of Lucy and Ryan populated my head. Their smiling faces, the sounds of their laughter—I watched them fade, slowly disappear. With all I had done, with all the precautions taken, this was the punishment for failure. Every hurdle cleared only prompted another to appear.

My children were in Napa Valley. I was in the city. I couldn't magically teleport there. There was no genie offering me three wishes. But I could still try. I could dig out from under that mountain of hopelessness that was crushing me. I could get up off that floor, shed my last tear, shake off that empty feeling, and do what I do best.

Never give up.

Sei was gone. She had disappeared into the blanket of fog. All I had to work with was her message. It was clear yet confusing. Why turn on my family? Had the game changed again? Was I suddenly no longer the target? It made no sense. I was the thorn that had punched the holes in the mastermind's game. I was the one he should have been angry with. Or was this simply some sort of sick twist to the game, a way to test my will and my ability to save my children? I shook my head. Finding the answer to all those questions didn't matter. This was about saving my children. Could I get to them first?

Sei's message implied there was immediate danger, not something to come in the following days. If a hit had been ordered on them, the clock had just started. I had to move.

"Knox! Copeland!" I called out as I hurried down the stairs. "Get up!"

I quickly brought them up to speed on Sei's visit and departing message.

"Wait. Hold on," Knox said. His eyes shifted back and forth between Copeland and me. "We're not completely screwed here. There are two agents with your family, right? They can at least secure the place until we can get there."

I nodded.

"Napa Police—we should alert them," Copeland said.

"There's risk with that. I highly doubt they have the experience to handle a situation like this. We'll use them another way. Have them set up roadblocks. Maybe we can catch Sei before she reaches the B&B."

"Abby, what was she wearing?" Copeland asked. "Tell me everything so I can brief NPD on who they're looking for."

I thought briefly about what Knox had said. Could we really stop her from reaching the B&B? Was it even possible?

"Abby?" Copeland's voice sounded louder this time. "We don't have time here."

As I scrolled through my address book for Castro's number, it hit me. "It's not Sei," I said.

"What do you mean it's not her? You just told us—"

"She wants us to think it's her, but it's not."

Knox shook his head and let out a breath of frustration. "I'm not following you."

"The threat is already there."

"Wait, are you saying it's the owners of the B&B? Because if you are—"

"It's not them. It's one of our own."

Castro sat on the edge of his bed in his dark room. He put his smartphone down, the light still visible on the screen. He had his orders, but things were moving fast. He'd barely had time to process what Kane had said; there was a hit on the kids, and Lin was the threat. The mastermind had infiltrated the FBI.

Kane hadn't had time to get into a lengthy explanation of how and why but asked that Castro not question her and get Po Po and the kids out of there. Time was of the essence. It was an hour's drive from the city to the B&B in Napa Valley. It would make no difference if agents were dispatched from the Oakland office; they were no closer. He was on his own for at least an hour.

From the second Castro had received the message, he had cycled through a number of scenarios, all of which were theoretically viable. But he could only choose one. And it had to be fast. And quiet. He thought through the option of demobilizing Lin, the one thing Kane had stressed that he not do. "He's too dangerous." Without knowing the full scope of the situation, Castro relinquished the thought.

He grabbed his weapon and double-checked the magazine. He pocketed another just in case before holstering his weapon and picking up the keys to the black Suburban parked outside.

He moved over to the door and placed his ear against it but heard nothing. Castro's bedroom was located on the second floor of the three-story building. A total of four rooms were available. His floor housed three double rooms, while a family-sized room/apartment took up the entire third floor. That was where Ryan, Lucy, and Po Po were staying. The suite had a fairly large living area and two separate bedrooms, each with its own full bath. The Fultons lived in a bungalow behind the B&B.

Castro exited his room and moved into the hallway. The entire building was constructed mostly of wood, including the flooring. Creaks were unavoidable. He walked slowly down the hall, his weapon held close against his thigh and out of view. Lin's room was at the far end, past the staircase. He paused slightly, listening, before turning right and heading up the half-landing staircase.

The stairs led directly to a decorative paneled door. Castro knew the door would be locked, and it didn't matter, because when they first arrived at the B&B, part of his security requirement was that the Fultons provide him with a key to the suite.

He removed the key ring from his pocket, inserted one of the brass keys into the five-pin cylinder of the deadbolt lock, and turned the key. The bolt slid out of the doorframe, emitting a clacking sound. With the knob turned, he pushed the door open. As usual, the fog had rolled in that night, masking most of the moonlight that would have shown through the windows of the suite, but his eyes had fully adjusted at that point. Castro slipped inside, stopping just short of shutting the door behind him. He had heard a faint but unmistakable sound. A floorboard had creaked on the second level. *Lin!*

Chapter 38

"We need to be right on this, Abby," Knox said. "Lin is an agent. Are you sure it's him?"

"Look, the Triads control the game. If they were able to get a guy on the inside, he most likely would be Chinese. They're wary of outsiders. They like to deal with their own."

Yeah, I racially profiled, but with good reason. Lin had never given me any indication in the past that he was bad. He seemed courteous, professional at all times, and by all accounts, he seemed to be a nice guy. But if what my gut told me were true, then that would have made perfect sense. The most dangerous enemy is the one that is never considered.

We quickly geared up with bulletproof vests and extra magazines for our handguns. I had found my weapon on the counter near the bathroom. Copeland grabbed the two assault rifles we kept on the premises, and we exited the tong.

"It normally takes an hour to get up to Napa, but I'll do my best to get us there in forty-five minutes," Knox promised as we headed toward our vehicle.

196   *Coit Tower*

I wasn't able to put a call into Kang until we were already packed into the SUV and heading out of the city. We were moving as fast as we could.

"Lin? Sheesh. I'm on my way, Abby. Do you want me to alert Napa Police?"

"Copeland is already on it. We're having them set up checkpoints a half mile away from the B&B."

"Good idea. We'll need all the help we can get."

My next call went to Reilly to keep him abreast of the latest developments and to see if there were agents we could tap into who might be closer than we were.

"I'm unaware of any agents that live in the Napa Valley locale," he said. "Agent House is in Oakland, but I would guess the distance is about the same. I'll still ask her and a few other agents to assist. Abby, I'm sorry this is happening."

I appreciated Reilly's concern, but a part of me resented him at the same time. I should have been there with my family. I knew what had happened wasn't his fault, but it angered me. I felt helpless. What kind of mother works a job that puts her family in harm's way? *Apparently me.*

But let's be honest here: I hadn't been thinking about children when I decided on this career path. Kids just weren't part of the equation. I doubted I even would have considered it had I known I would be raising them by myself. But I fell in love with a man who already had two children. At the time I thought, *We can do this. We're a team.* But six months later when he was murdered, that partnership ended, and suddenly I was a single mother with an unforgiving job. That was the hand I had been dealt, and all I could do was deal with it the best I could. Don't get me wrong; it wasn't easy. In the beginning, there were days I wanted to give up and walk away. But I didn't. It's easier now, but those thoughts still creep back into my head every now and then. I try to remember that every day forward is an opportunity to be better as a mother. Every parent is learning, not just me. At least, that's what I tell myself.

From the time we left the tong until we arrived at the B&B, I had been in contact with my mother-in-law via text message. Before I alerted Castro about the threat, I had called her and given her specific instructions. "Do not open the door for Agent Lin."

"Abby, I don't understand. What's happening?"

"He can't be trusted. Just get over to the kids' room and lock the door. Keep them quiet. Don't wake them if possible. Wait for Agent Castro. I'm on my way now."

I told Po Po only what she needed to know, not wanting to scare her any more than I already had. Fortunately, the kids were still sound asleep, oblivious to the danger just outside their bedroom door. After that call, she kept me updated with text messages.

The Fultons' B&B was located about a half mile south from where Highway 12 intersected with Highway 29. NPD had already set up two checkpoints but hadn't much to report. What little traffic passed through were locals the officers personally knew.

Behind us, a slew of news vans followed. Walking out of the tong wearing bulletproof vests and carrying rifles had been a huge tell that something was up. Surely they were salivating at what appeared to be a new development in the Chasing Chinatown story.

We were traveling east on Highway 12 and about ten minutes away from the B&B. Even though it was early morning and the roads were mostly empty, Knox had done a great job at shaving even more time off the drive. Still, it felt as though the vehicle couldn't move fast enough. I was a restless mess buckled in the front seat.

"You sure you're up for this?" Knox asked, keeping his eyes focused on the road ahead. "We can enter the building first."

I knew what Knox was implying. I didn't even want to think about it. We were talking about my family. There was no way I was sitting this one out, regardless of what might be waiting for us.

"I'm going in first," I said as we approached Highway 29.

Chapter 39

All at once, Castro's skin buzzed to life. The neurons in his brain fired as he worked to weigh his next move. There was only one reason Lin would be awake at this hour. Kane had been right.

Castro checked his watch. Eight minutes had passed since his last contact with her, and a mere thirty seconds were all that separated him from Lin. He thought about the few minutes he'd spent in his room, desperately trying to make sense of what Kane had conveyed. *Lin is an assassin? What's he doing working for the FBI?* So many questions and no time for answers. If he had spent another thirty seconds contemplating what he had been asked to do, essentially to turn his back on a fellow agent, Lin would be in this room and not him.

First things first: secure the room. Initially he'd planned to move the family out of the B&B and drive away—an obvious no-go with Lin on the move. Castro had already flipped the deadbolt on the door, the first line of defense. He thought of rearranging the furniture in front of the door but passed on the idea—too loud and not very effective.

Rather than face Lin, Castro started to look for another way out of the building. As he hurried over to one of the large windows to see if it were possible to climb out and make it to the ground, common sense reared its head. *I have an elderly woman and two young children. What the hell am I thinking?*

Castro had come to grips with what had fast become a reality: The door was the only way out of the suite. That would undoubtedly put him on a collision course with Lin. His only real option would be to secure the family as best he could and wait for backup to arrive. It was doable, except for one small hiccup: Castro had never counted on Lin having a key to the room.

He could hear the mechanism of the lock cylinder turning. He could hear the latch receding out of the doorframe. He could hear the click of the door opening. There wasn't any time to think, only to act.

Castro moved toward the backside of the opening door. Lin would have to open the door all the way and move into the room in order to spot him. By then, Castro would have had numerous opportunities to pull the trigger if it came to that.

But what if Kane was wrong?

The thought weighed on Castro like two monster-sized anvils. This was an FBI agent, someone who, like him, had taken an oath to uphold the law, to support and defend the Constitution of the United States against all enemies, foreign and domestic. Were there ever any bad agents in the FBI's history? Sure. But Kane had fingered Kip Lin. He might have been new to the service—a rookie, really—but Castro had known Lin for three months before he had received the assignment to secure Kane's family, and he felt like he had gotten to know the guy.

On top of that, Castro had been in the service for a good fifteen years. He liked to think that, over those years, he'd developed a sixth sense when it came to vetting people. Could he have gotten it wrong? Or had Kane? Suggesting that Lin was a bad egg without any solid evidence was alarming. It's not something that an agent readily accepts. An agent has to trust his partner with his life—and up until then, Castro had seen no reason not to trust Lin.

Still, Castro granted Kane the benefit of the doubt. She was an outstanding agent and, as far as he knew, about as straight as they came. But that's not what had him drawing a gun on another agent. It was her phone call, something about her voice, the way it quivered and how it cracked on some of her words. It was uncharacteristic of Agent Kane. It was fear.

Chapter 40

Castro waited with his Glock aimed at the door, his finger resting inside the trigger guard. He had already decided that, if Lin entered the room with his weapon drawn, he would order him to drop it first. One warning. One opportunity.

The door swung all the way open. Castro didn't dare move to give away his location. He stood off to the side of a small sofa with his knees slightly bent, his arms straight out in front, and his weapon trained on the doorway.

He waited for what seemed an abnormally long time for Lin to enter the room. It had Castro wondering if Lin knew he was waiting just behind the door. But how could he? Castro slept light and kept the ringer volume on his cell on low, so no way Lin had heard it ring. Castro had also been careful about his movements throughout the building. Surely the two creaks in the floorboards his footsteps had caused hadn't been enough to penetrate Lin's door.

Castro thought briefly about calling out to Lin but nixed that idea. Instead, he took a step to the right and paused. He continued this action until he could clearly see outside the door. He saw nothing.

As he took a step forward, he felt a sharp pain in his chest near his right shoulder. Seconds later, the same agonizing pain exploded in his right biceps, crippling his arm and leaving just his left hand to hold his gun. He moved to raise his right arm but couldn't. The pain stifled him, and he knew why. Protruding from his arm was the handle of a small knife.

He was being attacked.

Like lighting, two more knives struck him, one in his left thigh and one in his left arm. A soft groan left his lips. He lost the grip on his weapon, and it fell to the wooden floor, clacking away from him. Castro's left leg buckled from the pain, but he prevented himself from falling completely. He rested on one knee with his other leg straight out, only to see Lin charging at him. Castro had no defense.

Castro lay on his back as his partner, the man he had called a friend, straddled him. He felt the cool metal of a blade pressed against his neck.

"Don't make a sound," Lin whispered, his breath hot against Castro's cheek. His eyes were dark, but their intensity shined brightly.

Castro could not bite his tongue. "Why?"

A grin widened on Lin's face. "Why? Don't take it personally. This is business. I'm being paid to do a job. That's all."

"Paid? Who's paying you? They're just children. Have

you no conscience?"

"My employer is of no concern. Of course, the mother-in-law is safe. She's not part of the contract. Nor were you, Marty. You should have stayed in your room. I imagine a convoy of black SUVs is racing toward the B&B right about now. Yes, I realize Agent Kane has been tipped off, though I have no idea how she figured out that I was the threat. Did she tell you? That's why you're up here, right? Kane contacted you."

"She didn't get into the details."

"You know, it's part of the plan—that Agent Kane arrives here just in time to discover that she's too late to save her kids. Sick, yeah, I know, but I don't ask questions. I'm just here to collect a paycheck."

Lin pressed the knife into Castro's neck and pulled away, easily slicing through his vocal chords and severing his jugular. Lin pressed his palm tightly against Castro's mouth until the man stopped moving beneath him. He then ran both sides of the blade over Castro's shirt before standing.

I wonder which room the kids are in. I'd hate to accidentally walk into Po Po's room and have to kill the old woman.

Lin took a step forward toward the bedroom door behind Castro, thinking he would have guarded the door the kids were behind. He had only taken one step before a noise alerted him.

Lin spun around, arm cocked back and ready to release the knife, but stopped short of throwing it. "You?"

Chapter 41

Lin spoke in a hushed yet direct tone. "Don't tell me the plan has changed, because clearly…" He waved a hand at Castro's lifeless body.

Sei stepped out from the doorway. Her arms hung relaxed at her sides, and her facial features were neutral. There was nothing threatening about her approach, and there wasn't any reason for Lin to be worried anyhow. He had met Sei in Shanghai just before he'd set off for training at Quantico.

Lin was a different type of assassin from Sei; he was manufactured. The mastermind had recruited a young mercenary with raw talent and a whole lot of promise and then groomed him into an intelligent, highly trained killing machine.

In exchange for this, Lin had but one duty to fulfill for the mastermind: join the ranks of the FBI and remain there until the Chasing Chinatown game had completed its run. If he were utilized for tasks during that time, he would be adequately compensated.

Upon the completion of the game, their arrangement would end, and he would no longer be in the mastermind's employ. He would be free to remain at the FBI or leave. Lin thought it was easy money and a trade-off that favored him. Achieving FBI status would give him unprecedented access that many people around the world would pay him handsomely for. He hadn't thought his services would ever come into play. But they had.

He lowered his arm while his brow did a terrible job of masking his confusion. *Why is she even here?* He didn't report to her, and he had clearly understood his orders from the mastermind. He even thought that maybe he had gotten it wrong but quickly ditched that notion, as he had never gotten an assignment wrong. Unless… "Just to be clear here, this is my contract, my payday."

"This isn't about money. The job has been canceled," Sei said calmly.

"Protocol states that only the boss can cancel a hit. Why was I not contacted directly?"

Lin glanced at his watch and then snapped his fingers three times. "Time's running out. I need to finish the job." He turned around and headed toward the bedroom door.

NPD had set up the checkpoint where Highway 29 and Highway 12 intersected. That's where we cut our ties to the media caravan following us and ordered them to wait at the checkpoint until further notice. The captain in charge radioed his men at the other checkpoint and gave them the go-ahead to move in.

A trail of blue and red lights lit up the highway as we sped toward the B&B. A few minutes later, Knox hooked the steering wheel to the left, and the SUV made a sharp turn onto a dirt road leading into the property. I could barely make out the building as we approached. During the day, I imagined it would be partly visible through a couple of trees, but the fog that night had masked it fairly well.

House had called to say that she and another agent were about ten minutes out. I told her we were at the B&B and would move to enter the building immediately. I didn't want to wait. I couldn't.

There were six agents in total and about a dozen officers from NPD, more than enough manpower. NPD would work to set up a perimeter and secure the property to prevent anybody from slipping away while we breached the building.

I texted Po Po to let her know we were there and asked if she heard voices outside the door. She said no but couldn't be sure.

That fact that she still texted me was good news, though we were heading in with the idea that Lin was still in the house. If he wasn't, Castro would have reached Po Po and the children and gotten them out. Instead, Castro had gone silent and stopped communicating. Something had gone wrong.

A few of NPD's vehicles were equipped with battering rams. We stacked up behind Copeland, and he splintered the front door of the B&B. One by one, we filed into the foyer and fanned out.

I knew the kids and Po Po were on the top floor and both Lin and Castro were on the second. Knox ordered a couple of agents to clear the second floor while the rest of us headed up the stairs.

We stacked up behind Copeland on the landing at the top of the staircase. From down below, we could hear still hear voices calling out, "Clear." Copeland gave a whispered count to three before throwing the ram into the door and destroying it. I went in first.

Upon entry, I noticed two motionless bodies on the carpet. With my weapon trained on them, I called out, "Po Po!" and headed toward the room I knew they should be in.

Knox moved toward securing the other bedroom. Copeland made a beeline for the two bodies to assess if they were still a threat.

I knocked on the door. "It's me. Open up."

A few seconds later, the lock clicked, and the door opened.

Chapter 42

I let out a breath of relief when I counted three familiar faces in the room. Lucy wasted no time running toward me and jumping into my arms. Holding her, I gave Ryan and Po Po a healthy dose of hugs and kisses.

"Mommy, what's happening?" Lucy asked. "Why do we have to leave? Its still nighttime."

From the sound of Lucy's voice, I could tell that she wasn't aware of what had happened. "I know, sweetie, but we have to move again."

"Are we going home now?"

"No, not just yet."

I pulled Ryan back against my side. "How are you?" I asked, unsure of what he knew. I assumed he had an idea because even I could see the police cruisers with their flashing lights through the windows.

Knox spoke through the door. "Everything okay in there?"

"We're fine," I answered.

"The situation is covered out here, literally."

I assumed Knox meant he had gone ahead and covered the bodies, knowing I still had to get the kids out of the building. I already had a good guess that the bodies belonged to Castro and Lin. I had recognized their body shapes. *Had I been wrong about Lin? Was there someone else?*

I spent the next few minutes enjoying my family before having to do the inevitable. The B&B was a crime scene, and I needed to remove them from it.

The lights in the living room were still off, and Knox and Copeland helped escort us down a path that wouldn't have Ryan or Po Po stepping over a body. I had Lucy in my arms and shielded her eyes. I don't think she had any idea of what we were walking past.

Ryan, on the other hand, probably knew what lay under those sheets. From the moment Castro and Lin had moved into our house, he'd understood the situation. He never once had let on that he was bothered by any of this, but I couldn't know for sure. Still, I felt guilty. *I should look into counseling for the family.*

Once outside, Knox and Copeland walked us over to the SUV we had arrived in. We bumped into House on the way.

"Abby, thank God everyone is okay."

"We're all good," I said as I ushered the kids and Po Po into the backseat of the vehicle, locking the door behind me.

House knew Lin had been fingered as a possible threat but hadn't had a chance to enter the B&B. I gave her the lowdown of what I had seen on the third floor, but I couldn't yet speak for the other floors, other than saying they appeared to be empty.

"Castro? Lin? Both dead?"

"I couldn't see their faces, but I'm pretty sure it's them up there."

She shook her head. "This makes no sense. That means there was a third person."

I nodded. I called two officers over to the vehicle and asked them to watch over my family while House and I went back inside for more answers.

The lights in the suite were on, and Knox and Copeland were standing near the bodies, talking softly amongst themselves. They had pulled the sheets back, and House and I could clearly see that it was Castro and Lin lying on the floor.

Before I could say anything, Knox spoke, his voice solemn and matching his body posture. "From what we can tell, Castro has three blades of some kind sticking out of him. Throwing knives are my guess. They were probably used from a distance to immobilize him but not enough to kill him. His neck is severed. Pretty sure that's what did him in."

House and I moved in closer. I bent down and looked at Lin. I didn't need a play-by-play from Knox. I could see a knife handle sticking out from one side of his neck, the tip protruding from the other side. I leaned in for a better view before looking up. "I think I know who the third person is."

Chapter 43

Earlier in the night, when I had filled in Knox and the others about Sei's visit, I left out a few details. "The knife in Lin's neck looks a lot like the knife she had hanging from her hip. At least, the size is dead on."

"This is getting stranger by the minute," Knox said, running his hand across his face. "We have an assassin who warns you about your children being in danger and then shows up and kills Lin… Heck, she might have killed both of them for all we know."

"Well, maybe she was here to kill the kids, but Lin and Castro intercepted her." House looked at me, her eyes widely suggestive. "You said you warned Castro, right? Well, maybe the two were up here to protect the kids when they were attacked."

"Why not finish the job?" Copeland jumped in. "No offense here, Abby, but it wouldn't take much to get it done."

House crossed her arms over her chest. "Maybe the sound of the sirens approaching scared her off."

Knox chewed on his lip and started shaking his head. "Doesn't make sense. A trained assassin would have finished the job. And I agree with Copeland: She had time."

I listened to the possible scenarios that my fellow agents were tossing out. All of them had some sort of plausibility. Pegging Lin as the threat was a gut instinct; I could have been wrong. Maybe Sei warned me as a challenge. Could she get here before I did? I also found the situation confusing. "He's wearing gloves." I motioned at Lin with my head. "What agent do you know that wears gloves while on duty?"

Heads nodded in agreement.

"I think Castro got up here first, and then Lin surprised him." I walked over to the doorway. "Castro is standing over where his body is. Maybe he's walking toward the room where the children are when Lin enters the suite. Castro turns around, sees him, and draws his weapon—but not before Lin hits him with the knives." I pretended to throw knives. "Stunned, Lin moves in"—I walked over to the body—"and finishes the job."

"But this is all still based on the theory that Lin worked for the mastermind," Knox countered.

I bent down near Lin and pointed at one of his gloved hands. "I'm betting that's Castro's blood."

"There might be prints on that knife sticking out of Lin's neck. Tying it to Sei is still questionable, though," House added.

"So Lin finishes Castro, but before he can make a move on the kids, Sei shows up and kills him?" Knox asked.

"I know what you're thinking. 'Why?'" I stood up and rested my hands on my hips. "I can't say exactly why, but it might just be that the game is unraveling. I mean, it really has been ever since we started investigating. Changing the game to target me is a prime example. Add that the local management for the game had been targeted and removed, well, it's not the same game we first discovered."

"It certainly sounds like a lot of damage has been done," Copeland agreed.

"Still, that doesn't quite answer why Sei killed Lin," I said.

"It might be as simple as a squabble between two assassins, you know, fighting over a contract or something," House suggested.

Kang appeared right then. "I talked to Po Po and the kids before coming up. I'm really sorry this happened," he said, giving my arm a friendly squeeze.

I quickly brought him up to speed on what we had just been discussing. He took it all in without saying a word and glanced over the bodies before kneeling near Castro. He studied one of the blades sticking out of his thigh.

"I've seen a couple of shops in Chinatown selling those types of knives," I said.

"Yeah, these are common throwing knives, mostly sold for show. But these knives were not bought in Chinatown."

"What makes you say that?" I asked.

216 *Coit Tower*

"You see this?" He pointed at an engraving on the handle. "There was another character painted on the teapot we found in the tong. This one."

"Are you sure?"

"Positive."

"What does it mean?"

Kang stood up and let out a loud breath. We all stared at him, waiting for an answer.

"Well, I doubt any of you will believe me. Even I didn't believe it at first and had to triple check my research, but this character roughly translates into something known as Vagabond Kung Fu."

We all had the same look on our faces: blank.

"I wouldn't say it's a matter of believability," I finally said, "but more that we've never heard of it."

"Most people haven't because its whole existence is rooted in folklore. It might just be an overzealous assassin paying homage to a myth."

"Well, either way, you said the same character was on the teapot, right?"

"Yup, and that's where it gets tricky. It's clear that Sei is the mystery person who lived on the top floor of the tong. That means the teapot most likely belonged to her. If these throwing knives were used by Agent Lin, that's two separate people owning items with that character mark. That's not coincidence."

"So you're saying they're from the same school of

assassins?" Knox asked with a slight smirk.

Kang turned toward him. "That would make sense. As the story goes, Vagabond Kung Fu is a form of martial arts practiced by beggars or nomads that made their living from street performances that often involved acrobatics and rudimentary magic."

"Sort of like the Gypsies of Europe," Knox suggested.

"Yeah. These bands of wanderers were often victims of crime or were busy committing them. Either way, it's the reason why they developed this style of kung fu. It's a melding of the most deadly of Northern and Southern techniques. These beggars were often recruited as mercenaries because of those very skills."

"Acrobats? Magic? Sounds like ninjas," Copeland chuckled.

"Like I said, it's supposedly just folklore. Many believe that the *shinobi* or 'ninjas'"—Kang used air quotes to emphasize the word—"got their inspiration from Vagabond Kung Fu. Now, I'm not suggesting they didn't exist; they definitely did. There's documentation of clans existing as early as the Eastern Dynasty."

"So what are you saying? This knowledge was passed on through the years?"

Kang nodded. "Pretty much. It also developed further into what was considered the Black Arts, fanciful stuff like casting spells and witchcraft."

"Sounds like Harry Potter bullshit," Knox interrupted.

"But it also included skills ranging from simple pickpocketing to assassination," Kang continued. "That's the area where it continued to thrive as far as I understand it."

"So Lin and this Sei girl were tied together through this Vagabond Kung Fu?"

"Like a secret society," I said. "Maybe the mastermind is also one of these practitioners. It also helps to connect the dots between the game and the Triads. Maybe within the Triads, these secret mercenaries exist."

"Wouldn't you have heard about it with all the time you spent in Hong Kong?" House asked.

"You'd think, but I didn't." I looked at Kang. "What do you think?"

"It's easy to keep something hidden when it's widely considered to be nothing more than good, old-fashioned storytelling, especially within the Triads. From the Chinese point of view, they're compared to the Illuminati."

Knox rubbed his forehead. "I don't know, guys. Ninjas, secret societies, mythological kung fu: this is a bit too much. Do we really think this stuff matters, even if there is some truth to it?"

"If it helps to answer the 'why,' then yes, it could help," Kang said.

"So those two are part of the same secret group of assassins. Phhfftt… How does that help us put an end to the mastermind and get this bounty off Abby's head?"

Good question.

Chapter 44

"Drago!" Petrovic flung a pillow at the sleeping man's head, hitting him square.. "Wake up!"

Zoric lifted his head off the pillow slightly. His eyes were crusted over, only one able to break the seal. Adrijana lay next to him completely under the covers and motionless, obviously still asleep.

"What time is it?" Zoric asked as he looked around.

"Look at what's on the TV!" Petrovic pointed at the flat-screen that had CNN showing.

Zoric rubbed his eyes and propped himself up on an elbow for a better look. A reporter was covering the double murder at a B&B in Napa Valley.

"Two FBI agents are dead. Apparently, that is where they were hiding our target's family. We're fucked, I tell you. No way we can get near her now."

"Shut up!" Zoric ordered as he scooted forward to the foot of the bed and listened to the reporter recap the events of the night.

"Another team struck while we were here sleeping like we're on some fucking holiday. We completely screwed up. I knew—"

"Shut up!" Zoric said again more intently as he leaned in, taking in the situation unfolding on the newscast.

By then, Adrijana had awakened and sat next to Zoric, watching with great interest. The live report had switched to Agent Kane making a statement earlier in the morning. A reporter had asked if the murders were the mastermind's doing. The three of them were surprised when they heard her answer.

"We have evidence to believe that Agent Lin worked for the mastermind. We alerted Agent Castro of the threat, but by the time we arrived, both agents were found dead. Agent Castro prevented Agent Lin from harming my family, but unfortunately, he succumbed to injuries sustained during that confrontation."

"Another team tried to get to the agent through her kids," Petrovic said.

Zoric wiped his hand across his mouth. "I don't think that was another team. The only way to get to Agent Kane through her kids is to kidnap them. What then? Ask for a ransom? Lure her into a trap? It's a stupid move. It would have never worked."

"So then why was this agent sent to attack her family?" Adrijana asked.

"I don't know, but I think somehow the mastermind is behind this move."

"You think the game is changing again?" Petrovic's voice rose, a barometer for his agitation. He threw both arms up before kicking the ottoman over.

"I think the sooner we make our move, the better," Zoric said.

"Now what?" Adrijana asked. "Security will be tight around that place. Surely they will know we're not real journalists."

Zoric clasped his thighs with his hands and kneaded the flesh a bit. "That's why we must wait for her at the tong. It'll be easy to blend in with the others. Eventually they'll come back, and that's when we'll strike."

Chapter 45

House and three other agents that I knew well took over duties to secure my family and move them back to our home. The premises had already been secured by Knox to the point that a presidential visit was viable. Reilly also ordered checkpoints to be established at either end of my street. Only residents would be allowed entry. I had complete confidence in House's ability to keep my family out of harm's way.

By the time we had left the B&B, it was nearly nine in the morning. We were heading back to the tong to determine our next steps. Interviewing Ethel would be a priority since we still hadn't had any solid leads regarding Charles Yee's whereabouts. Lots of calls from the public, but nothing had panned out. Even Kang's efforts to reach Yee via phone weren't helping—endless ringing, no voicemail. I wanted to push Ethel harder for her cooperation. She needed to understand the seriousness of the situation and that finding Yee had become the bureau's top priority. So far, he was most likely to be the mastermind or at least someone who could put us a step closer to him. Reilly had already dispatched two agents to bring her in for further questioning.

I rode back into the city with Kang. Knox and Copeland followed us in their SUV. "Look, Kyle, I know you think we're overreacting, but it's important that we have a heart-to-heart conversation with Ethel. Right now, she's our best bet at identifying Yee, even if it's only to provide a sketch artist with a description. We need to be circulating his picture."

"No, you're right. He's our number one suspect in this case, even if he is her friend. I know Ethel; she'll cooperate."

The deaths of Castro and Lin wouldn't have any effect on the tong serving as our command post and living quarters. It was business as usual and another opportunity for Sei to pay me a visit. At least, that was my hope.

I had a lot of questions and not a whole lot of answers. The pieces just didn't fit right. The question that got batted around in my head the most was why Sei had showed up at the tong to warn me about my children. It's not like she was an informant I had developed. We barely knew each other. Plus, she was a killer, and there was a big paycheck on my head. Let's not forget that very important detail.

As a whole, we were still undecided on whether she killed only Lin or both of them. CSI's investigation would hopefully shed some light on that. Either way, I wanted another conversation with her. Only this time, I wanted to make sure she couldn't leave.

Driving over the Golden Gate Bridge, my eyes wandered off toward the mouth of the bay and into the blue Pacific Ocean. The water was choppy and dotted with white peaks. A large container ship slowly made its way toward the bridge, escorted by four tugboats. Most of the morning fog had burned off, and the sun was beaming down. It was a beautiful sight.

"Never gets old, does it?" Kang said.

I blinked at him.

"The view," he added helpfully.

I nodded slowly, still lost in my thoughts. I was heading back to the tong when I should have been heading home with my family. The mother in me screamed at my selfishness. However, the agent in me countered. My family and I would never be safe until we caught the mastermind. Working the case instead of staying with them was a necessary but unpopular decision.

When we turned onto Waverly Place, Kang promptly drove up onto the sidewalk and parked right outside the tong. The area had unofficially been designated as our parking spot. A few news vans were still camped out along the street, though most had followed us to Napa. I expected they'd all eventually make their way back to Chinatown or split duties between both locations. The double murder at the B&B had become the hot story.

Before we could enter the tong, a woman and two men approached us. She spoke with a European accent. "Excuse me, Agent Kane. Could you spare fifteen minutes for an interview?"

"Sure. Who are you guys with?" I asked as I looked toward the two news vans.

"Oh, we're with a small news service in Serbia. We are here to cover the investigation."

"Serbia?"

"Our government doesn't want CNN to be the only source of world news. Our van is that one at the far end of the street." She pointed. "We can conduct the interview inside."

"Nah." I needed to freshen up first. "Follow me. There's a small office on the second floor that I've been using as a media room."

I held the door open for the trio. "Come on. I don't have all day." Everyone else had already headed inside except for Kang, who paced the sidewalk a few feet away. He was talking on his cell and motioned for me to go ahead without him.

I led the news crew up to the media room on the second floor and told them to make themselves comfortable and that I would be back in a few minutes. I then went up to my floor to splash some water on my face. Knox and Copeland were already up there looking at the boards. While their assignment was my security, they had obviously taken an interest in the investigation and were working it alongside me. I didn't mind. I needed the help. "I'll bang out this interview quickly and join you guys when I'm done."

I returned to the second floor. The meeting room I had been utilizing was small, maybe twelve feet by twelve feet. It was furnished with a small, round table and four chairs with an old wooden credenza against the wall. It was windowless and probably not the most comfortable place in the building, but it served my purpose; I didn't want the interviews to be longer than needed.

As I walked toward the room, I could see the woman sitting at the table, smiling at me. The taller, skinner man operating the camera stood off to the side, but the other male, the shorter, bulkier one, remained hidden from my view. "Sorry about the wait," I called out before entering the room.

"Are you going to be at the B&B covering the double murder?" Kang asked into his cell phone.

"No, another crew got that assignment. I'm stuck in Chinatown," Suzi said, her tone clearly indicating that she had a pout on her face.

"Hey, it's not that bad. I'm here. We can grab lunch together."

"I guess." Her voice warmed slightly. "What's happening there now?"

"Nothing really. We just got back. Abby's giving an interview to a news crew, and I'm not sure what the other agents are doing."

"Which news channel?"

"They're foreigners. I think they said they were from Serbia. I guess this case is bigger than I thought."

"Why aren't they at the B&B? That's where the story is."

"Not sure. Maybe they were for a little bit. So what time do you think you'll get here?"

"I don't know. Gary should have picked me up about an hour ago, but he's late and not answering his phone. I swear, he'll be the reason I get fired. He's always late. I don't know how he even got this job. He's not even that great with the camera, always catching me when my guard is down and not looking my best. I have an image to uphold, you know? I…"

As Suzi went on and on about Gary, Kang dropped the phone down to his side, her yakking still ringing out loud and clear as if the phone were on speaker. He didn't know if a fresh pot of coffee had been brewed upstairs and decided to grab a cup from the restaurant on the corner. Just before he reached the entrance, he passed a news van. Painted in bold lettering on the side was KTVU Channel 2.

Recognizing the station, he put the phone back up to his ear. "Hey, Suzi. …Suzi!"

"Why are you interrupting me?"

"You said Gary was supposed to pick you up a while ago, right?"

"Yeah."

"Well, I'm standing next to a KTVU news van right now. I'm pretty sure it's the same beat-up van that he drives you around in."

"What? Are you sure? Wait, look inside the window. Do you see little rubber Smurfs sitting on the dashboard?"

Kang stepped closer to the passenger's side door and peered inside.

Crap! Abby!

Chapter 46

Kang pocketed his phone and drew his weapon in one fluid movement before racing toward the front entrance of the tong. *How could I have let this happen? Why didn't I check their news credentials?* The team entrusted to keep Kane safe had gotten sloppy, and Kang worried they were in danger of paying the price.

It didn't take much more for Kang to piece together that the journalists were impostors. The only piece of the puzzle left was whether Kane was still alive.

Up the first flight of stairs he bounded, his heart pumping out a resounding bass line in his chest. With his weapon out front, he pivoted on the small landing between the first and second floor. From there, he kept his steps light and his movement minimal. He didn't know if he was walking into an ambush. He couldn't save Kane if he was injured, or worse, dead.

The tong was quiet, and he wasn't sure whether that was good news or bad news. He hoped it wasn't the latter. *Where are Knox and Copeland? Maybe they're with Abby?* Thinking that there might not have been an opportunity yet for the team to strike was a positive thought that Kang steadily clung to.

He stopped short of the last step to the second floor. The stairs led to an open space—the recreation room. Kang knew Kane had been using one of the offices to conduct her interviews. He peeked around the corner, his gun leading the way. The rec room was empty. After a few steps to the right, he could see that the kitchen was empty too. The larger of the two offices was to the left. The door was open, but the smaller one, farther past the kitchen, had its door closed.

Kang knew it was tight quarters in there. Busting down the door wasn't a smart move. *Think, dammit! Think!* He thought about rallying the other agents, but his gut told him if he didn't act now, it would be too late. Plus, he didn't know where they were. A slew of options entered his brain, each no better than the other. *Pick one, Kyle. You don't have all day.* He did and hoped he had chosen wisely.

"Abby," he called out. He stood about fifteen feet from the door. "There's another news team that wants to conduct an interview. Shall I bring them up?" Maybe if the team knew someone was outside the door but not a threat, they would answer, or better yet, she would answer.

Silence.

"Abby?" He tried once more. The seal of the door cracked, and Kang quickly holstered his weapon and put a smile on his face. The shorter of the two males slipped out through a narrow opening, but Kang wasn't able to see inside the room from where he stood before the door was closed.

The man wore gray slacks and a blue sweater and walked toward Kang with his right hand extended. A smile lit up his round face. "I'm Marko, the producer," he said, his voice lowered. His ice-blue eyes bore into Kang, never straying. "Abby is on camera now. We should finish in ten minutes. I'll notify you when we're done, okay?"

Kang played along and shook Marko's hand graciously. His hands were rough. *Odd for an office worker type of job*, he thought. He had a good foot of height on the barrel-chested man. As Marko's grip loosened, Kang made his move.

He latched onto the producer's hand and yanked. At the same instant, Kang's left hand shot up and connected with the man's thick neck. Instantly, Marko gasped and choked. He struggled to regain his breath, but Kang didn't let up. He followed with a head butt so forceful that surely the others in the office had heard the thump.

Marko lost consciousness, and blood trickled from both nostrils. Kang caught him and lowered him quietly to the floor before slapping a pair of handcuffs on him. *You live. Lucky you.*

Kang drew his weapon again. *Two more to go.* He called out once more, hoping to further his ploy. "All right. Thanks, Marko." He then walked toward the office, allowing his footsteps to be heard. He needed the others to believe that Marko had gotten rid of him and was returning to the room. He stopped an arm's reach away from the door and grabbed hold of the knob.

He pulled the door open as quickly as possible and brought his gun up. Standing in front of him was the taller of the two men with his back turned. He was operating the camera. He couldn't see the woman, but that didn't matter. Kang pulled the trigger, and the man's head jerked forward a bit. A poof of pink sprayed the air just before he dropped to the floor, revealing Kane.

She was seated in a chair on the other side of the table with her mascara smeared under her left eye. Silver duct tape covered her mouth. Standing next to her was the last of them, the woman, and she held a large hunting knife against Kane's neck.

Kang didn't think. He didn't wait to confirm. He pulled the trigger again. The round struck the woman in the right cheek, and she fell back against the wall, losing her grip on the knife. She cried out in pain, and Kang fired again, striking her forehead. The woman went silent and crumpled to the floor.

Kang rushed over to Abby and peeled the tape off her mouth.

She gasped twice for air before saying, "What the hell took you so long?"

Chapter 47

Kang untied my hands, and I brought them around front and rubbed life back into my wrists.

"You okay?" he asked, brushing a few strands of hair out of my eyes.

"Yeah, as soon as I entered the room, the producer—Marko was his name? Anyway, he grabbed me from behind, and the other two helped to subdue me. They had me tied up and gagged within seconds." I stopped rubbing. I could see the guilt pouring from Kang's eyes. "Hey, now, I didn't see it coming either."

"We could have prevented this."

"Tell me about it."

I heard the sound of footsteps clomping down the stairs.

"Abby!" Knox called out.

"We're in here."

"Damn! What the hell happened?"

I still had my butt planted in the chair, but I could see Knox and Copeland standing near Marko with their weapons drawn.

"Another team is what happened." I looked up at Kang.

"Is he dead?"

He shook his head. "Careful," Kang called out. "That one's alive, but I can't say the same for the two in here."

Copeland bent down and searched the man. "No identification and no media pass."

Knox and Copeland approached the room but stopped at the doorway.

"I'll call this in," Copeland said after a quick glance at the bodies on the floor.

"Hold up," I said. "Let's not do that just yet. An army of agents and crime scene investigators will take the spotlight off the B&B. I want a few minutes of quiet time with the producer."

"Copeland, secure the front door. Nobody in. Nobody out," Knox said.

"Come on, Abby; let's get you out of here." Kang grabbed my hand and helped me step over the woman.

Once outside of the room, I felt as though I could finally breathe again. I walked toward a window that overlooked the street below and collected my thoughts. A lot had just happened, and somehow I had survived again. I was staring outside absentmindedly, still trying to comprehend what had just happened, when I felt a hand on my shoulder.

"Abby?"

I turned around and found Kang standing there with a glass of water for me. "Here, drink this."

236   *Coit Tower*

His eyes had a soft look, and his shoulders were a little droopy. I gave him a playful punch to the arm. "It's not your fault. We all missed it. I'm just glad you figured it out."

"*How* did you figure it out?" Knox asked as he joined us by the window. He removed his jacket and placed it over the back of a nearby chair.

Kang went on to tell us about the phone call he'd had with Suzi.

Knox had both hands resting on his waist. He shook his head. "If you hadn't taken that phone call… I mean, we got frickin' lucky here. I'm embarrassed that this even happened." His eyes caught mine. "I'm really sorry, Abby." Knox slapped Kang on the back. "You did a great job. Thank God you were here."

"I second that." I wrapped both arms around Kang's torso and gave him a long hug.

"That's three," he said.

"Huh?" I pulled my head away from his chest and looked up. He had that crooked smile on his face.

"Three times I saved your butt. It's becoming annoying."

"Puhhhlease." I snorted as I pushed away from him. My eyes rolled as if there were no tomorrow. "Methinks your math is wrong."

"What are you talking about? Okay, hold on." He held up a finger and began a count. "Just now—that's one. The tunnels underneath Chinatown—that's two. At your home with Team Favela—that's three."

"Whoa, whoa, whoa. Hold on, Masked Marvel. You can't count Team Favela. Technically, you just showed up after the fact."

Kang bounced his head from side to side. "Okay, so two. Still, I just wanted it on the record. So no more telling your trumped-up story of how you saved me."

Whenever someone asked how Kang and I had met, and a lot of people have, I would tell the story of how I caught a gang member he had been chasing, all while off duty, with a full belly and with my family in tow. Sure, I exaggerated the story to sound as though catching the guy saved Kang, but it got so many laughs, I couldn't help it. It was good material.

"I can't believe the two of you are arguing over something like this." Knox turned and walked back toward Marko, who appeared to be regaining consciousness. He rolled him over with his foot. "Hey, I got a story for you. You're in deep shit."

Marko's awaking refocused our attention. He was the first player from the game that we had apprehended alive.

Kang helped Knox lift Marko into a chair. His nose had stopped bleeding, and he breathed heavily through his mouth. "You broke my nose."

"You're lucky that's all that happened to you," Knox countered quickly. "Your friends over there got it worse."

Marko looked back toward the office and strained his neck for a better look before turning back toward us. "Where's Adrijana? Where is she?"

Nobody said a word, and Marko got his answer. What happened next wasn't something I had expected to see. The tough-looking Serbian broke down in tears. "You killed her?" He asked. "Why? She didn't do anything. She was a good girl."

"Who's the other guy, Marko?" Kang asked.

He didn't answer and continued to silently weep. His mouth hung open, and a strand of saliva stretched from his lower lip.

"Hey!" Knox said sharply. "We asked you a question."

Marko looked up. The whites of his eyes were red, and his eyelids were showing signs of puffiness. He then told us to fuck ourselves. That didn't go over well with Knox, who responded by slapping his face. "We can do this the hard way. I like the hard way."

As much as I wasn't a fan of this degenerate, I didn't think antagonizing him would get him to talk, and we needed him to talk.

I tapped Knox's arm and motioned to him with my eyes to let me try. I kneeled down next to the producer. "Marko, I'm sorry about Adrijana." Earlier, she'd told me her name was Ana. "That's a pretty name. Was she your girlfriend?"

He nodded. His gaze returned to the floor.

"It's unfortunate," I continued. "She's not here with us because of the game. The game is the culprit here. Help us put an end to it."

Marko raised his head. His eyes were glassy but focused.

"If it weren't for the game, Adrijana would still be alive. Tell us what you know."

"What do you want to know?" Marko said, his voice froggy.

"How about your real name for starters?" I asked, placing a comforting hand on his shoulder.

In the next several minutes, he spilled all the details about Team Balkan.

"How do you communicate with the people behind the game, Drago?"

"We send them messages, but the game isn't working like it used to."

"What do you mean?"

"Everything just stopped working. I don't know."

I looked over at Kang. "I guess we weren't the only ones who were cut off."

"So the team tracking, live updates, the map: all of it went dead?"

Zoric nodded.

"And you never met anybody from the game aside from the contacts that gave you the clues?"

He nodded again. Further questioning told us that

neither the address to the B&B nor that of my home was supplied to them.

"Where's Gary, the driver of the van?" Kang asked.

When Zoric told us about Petrovic killing the driver, Kang was obviously taken by surprise.

"Did they give you my name and address?" Kang prodded.

"We got your name from the news, and Adrijana used Google to find out where you live. She was smart with the online stuff."

"The media: a double-edged sword," Kang hissed. "I'll be back. I'm going to make a few calls, get a search started for the body."

Further questioning ran us into a dead end with Zoric. It seemed the other teams didn't know any more than we did. When I asked him about Sei, he responded by saying, "Who?"

I was ready to close the door on this chapter when I had an idea. It was a rehash, but it had helped the first time around.

Chapter 48

Knox and I moved quickly, knowing an army of agents and forensic specialists would eventually show up. I wasn't sure if we could pull it off, but we were willing to try. Before we could start, I had two questions for Zoric: What was the idea for my themed kill, and where was the phone they'd used to communicate with the game?

Zoric thought the first question was out of morbid curiosity and proudly told me their idea. Knox went to work and extracted the whereabouts of the phone along with the password. I think at that point, Zoric didn't care anymore. He resented being a part of the game. We handcuffed him to an old radiator that was bolted to the wall and got to work.

"I don't intend to disturb the crime scene." I walked back into the media room and reapplied the duct tape Kang had peeled off my mouth earlier. Next, I grabbed the KTVU microphone, flopped down on the table, and did my best to look as if I had died giving an interview. Knox snapped a picture with the phone we found on Petrovic.

"You sure this will work?" Knox asked as I logged on to the game.

"Well, the first time we posed as a team, we were

successful in playing for quite some time. But before we could upload our fake crime scene photos, we were discovered. The mastermind has no idea Team Balkan has been compromised. We have another opportunity here."

"Sounds like it's too good to pass up," Knox said.

"We have an advantage, though; I'm the Attraction. I mean, how on Earth would one of them be able to snap a photo of me like this if they hadn't been successful?"

I selected the photograph and hit the send button. A message appeared and told us the upload was complete.

"Now what?"

"We wait."

"Wait for what?" Kang asked as he approached us.

"Knox snapped a picture of me looking pretty dead, and I just sent it in to the game. We're officially playing as Team Balkan."

"We're back in the game!" Kang gave me a spirited high five. "It worked once. Why not a second time, right?"

"Say they buy it. That means Team Balkan wins. Game over, right? No more teams coming after you?" Knox asked.

"That's what I'm thinking," I said. "Had they gotten to me, they would have done exactly what we have done and then waited to see what happens next."

"I guess in a perfect world, the mastermind gives the submission a thumbs up, declares Team Balkan the winner, and pays out the prize money." Kang pocketed his hands. "Might be an opportunity to grab the mastermind then, though I doubt he'll be the one delivering the goods."

"A wire transfer seems more likely," Knox suggested. "We can set up a dummy account and follow the money."

"There's just one thing."

Knox and I both looked at Kang. "What's that?"

"You have to stay out of sight until this plays out. You're dead, remember?"

"He's right, Abby," Knox said. "And it has to start now. Nobody can have access to you, even agents at the bureau. We can't afford any leaks to the media. They can help us sell this."

I clucked my tongue as I thought about what they had said. "The only person who needs to be convinced of my death is the mastermind." I looked at Zoric, who was still sitting on the floor next to the radiator. "What we need to keep under wraps is Team Balkan. What happened here can't get out."

"But you still agree you need to stay out of sight should we get the thumbs up, right?" Kang tilted his head a bit and scrunched his brow.

"Yeah, but I don't think we need to sell it to the world."

"All right then. I'll head downstairs and help Copeland at the door," Knox said. "We'll need to keep the number of investigators in this building to a bare minimum. Abby, you should probably get on the phone with Reilly and bring him up to speed. He'll be instrumental in containing the scene."

I nodded. "What about him?" I asked, motioning to Zoric.

"I'll keep an eye on him," Kang volunteered. "Where do you think he'll be detained?"

"Knowing Reilly, he'll want supermax, most likely at ADX Florence in Colorado."

"Ah, the Alcatraz of the Rockies." Kang turned to Zoric. "It'll be like you never existed."

I headed upstairs, not especially overjoyed with having to tell Reilly that there were two more bodies. He'd already had to deal with the fallout, both internally and externally, that came with having two dead agents show up on his watch, not to mention one of them being a traitor.

The first few minutes of the call had me holding my phone a good distance from my ear. Fortunately, there was sanity in my plan. We had done this once before, and it had helped us shut the game down in San Francisco and take out Jing Woo, the Triad Dragonhead in charge of Chinatown. I think that was the only reason Reilly agreed to help keep a lid on what had happened at the tong that morning.

I called Po Po next. I think I dreaded that conversation more.

"What you mean you dead?" she asked.

"I'm not really dead. I'm pretending. It's just an elaborate trick."

She grunted. "When you come home?"

"Well, that's the tricky part. In order to make the bad

guys believe that I'm dead, I can't be seen. I'll have to stay in hiding but only for a few days."

She let out a long breath. "You explain to Lucy and Ryan."

"Of course I'll tell them, but I wanted you to know first."

Sometimes I think Po Po assumes I never think things through, but I couldn't really blame her. She and the children had gone through a lot, and she was the one stuck on the front lines when Ryan and Lucy had questions.

Also, these types of circumstances did nothing to improve my standing amongst her friends. I can only imagine the gossip sessions. I mean, not everyone gets a call from their daughter-in-law telling them to go along with her fake death. Never-ending fodder is what I provided. I'm sure I didn't come across as a saint.

Chapter 49

Reilly had CSI show up in unidentified vehicles and civilian clothes. He kept the crew small, and they used generic suitcases to bring their equipment into the building. To further help, Reilly announced a press conference at the B&B to keep the attention there. It even got the two news crews that were outside the tong to pack up and head to Napa. That would help when it came time to remove the bodies. It's pretty hard to hide a body bag on a gurney.

Timothy Green, the medical examiner, said it wouldn't be a problem to use an unmarked van for transport. He also said he could wait for an opportunity to move the bodies; forensically, it posed no threat to their portion of the investigation.

From the second floor window, I saw Green park his vehicle outside. I hurried downstairs to meet him at the entrance. "We appreciate your help with this," I said, holding the front door open.

"It's gotten worse, hasn't it?" he said with a lowered voice as he looked up and down the street.

"It has. The bodies are up on the second floor," I said as I closed and locked the door behind us.

"This has got to be taking a toll on you," he said, looking back over his shoulder as I followed him up the stairs.

"It's harder on my family."

Green stopped at the landing between floors. "What can I do to help? There must be something."

I smiled at Green. "You're helping right now."

"What? The unmarked van?" Green motioned with his head. "I meant outside of my job. What about the family? Where are they now? Do they need a place to stay?"

"It's very kind of you to ask. My mother-in-law and the kids are moving back home. The Bureau is doubling their security efforts. My entire street will be on lockdown."

"And you?" he asked as he reached out and placed a hand on my shoulder.

"I'll be fine, but I appreciate your concern."

Green held his position on the landing as he peered deeper into my eyes.

"I'm serious. Everything is okay."

A second later, Green removed his hand. "Well, as long as you're not relying on the SFPD for your safety." He turned and continued up the stairs. "You let me know, though. Nothing is out of the question."

By dusk, we had the tong cleared out, and I could come out from hiding. Knox had asked earlier if I'd wanted the other agents that had been staying at the tong to stick around. I didn't feel that we were facing the same realities of an attack then as we had before, so we agreed we could do without them.

Kang had Chinese food delivered from the corner restaurant, and we all gathered in the rec room on the second floor. CNN played on the television, and Kang had the food laid out on a table. We all pulled up chairs and sat.

Since I couldn't go home just yet, and hanging around the tong wasn't ideal, Kang suggested I stay at his place.

"I'm serious, Abby," he said as he slurped chow fun into his mouth. "I have plenty of room. It's no problem. I want you to be there."

It wasn't the intrusion part that had me hesitant. "Aren't you forgetting something?" I dished a helping of oyster chicken and pork fried rice onto my plate.

"What?"

"Suzi. You know, your girlfriend. Doesn't she live there too?" Kang had mentioned after we got back from Bangkok that Suzi had officially moved in, though she had practically been living there since her return to the Bay Area.

"She'll have to understand. Plus the guest room is on another floor if that helps you feel better."

"Hey, I'm fine. *She's* the one I'm worried about. We can't have her running her mouth about me being there. You know, I'm supposed to be dead."

Kang held up his hand to beat back the sarcasm that had begun to punctuate my replies. "Don't you worry about

Suzi. I can handle her."

The conversation around the dinner table paused as the four of us focused on shoveling food into our mouths. Kang had done a great job with the spread: pork fried rice, oyster chicken, beef chow fun, spicy tofu, beef and broccoli, kung pao shrimp, stir-fried veggies, steamed carp, and spring rolls. Chilling in the refrigerator was my favorite dessert: almond jelly. Way too much food, but Kang was like me; he always over-ordered.

Between bites, I continually checked Team Balkan's phone for an update. So far, we had heard nothing regarding our submission.

"How long does it take?" Knox asked as he noisily destroyed a spring roll.

"Well, in the past, feedback ranged from almost immediate to a few hours, but that's just based on our own interactions. I think if after a day or two we don't have an answer, we can safely assume the mastermind wasn't fooled. I think at that point we go public about taking down another team and how we're a step closer to shutting down the game."

"Yeah, spin this thing in our favor," Copeland managed to say while chewing.

We sat around discussing the case a bit more after dinner. Ethel still hadn't been located, which wasn't a good sign. Agents had been dispatched to both her home and the CCBA. They were now following up on known associates of hers. Kang had also placed numerous calls to her but got voicemail each time.

"Anything useful come back from NYPD on Yee?" I asked Kang.

He shook his head. "Nothing."

"I got the same result with our Tribeca office. They have no knowledge of him."

"Honestly, I'm worried." He leaned back in his chair and loosened his belt a notch. "This isn't in Ethel's character to just up and disappear. She's usually the center of attention, the one who is out socializing almost every night."

"Do you think maybe she's a little spooked by the investigation and our suspicions of Yee?" I asked.

"Probably. Most people would be." Kang checked his watch. "You ready to head back to my place?"

"Yeah. Just let me grab a few things. I'll be back down."

As I packed an overnight bag, I thought about how staying at Kang's place had dashed my hopes of receiving another nightly visit from Sei. For some reason, I'd just had it in my head that she would come back that night. The instinct wasn't based on anything concrete; I just wanted answers.

I thought briefly about leaving a note but decided not to. One, it would amount to inviting a dangerous person into Kang's place. Two, I had to stop thinking I had a friendly relationship with this woman. She hadn't come to me because she had thought we could become BFFs. There had been a reason, and it probably hadn't been a positive one. I shut the window and locked it. *Not tonight.*

Chapter 50

Knox and Copeland remained at the tong to help carry out our ruse. It was business as usual, except any requests for an interview with me were denied. The story they put out was that I had a sore throat and needed to refrain from any nonessential talking.

On the way over to Kang's place, I realized I had actually never been inside. I had met him outside numerous times, but that was about as far as I had ever gotten. He lived in an old Victorian with two floors instead of three like mine.

Kang held the front door open. "After you."

While neat and orderly, the décor was heavy on utilitarian and light on color and design. Blacks, whites, and blues dominated. Though there were signs of Suziness infiltrating his manly look: fresh flowers on a table near the entrance and a framed publicity photo of her hanging on the wall were two examples that stuck out.

"Come on, let me give you the tour."

The guest room, with its own bath, was located on the first floor. Suzi's influence continued with lavender walls and a matching floral duvet on the bed. A large, decorative mirror adorned a wall along with a collage of framed pictures and cute quotes. A light green wingback chair sat in the corner, and an antique dresser stood against another wall with a matching vanity next to it.

The bathroom smelled of fresh flowers and had the same light tones. White tiled floors and a dark, gray-and-black-tiled, step-in shower gave the bathroom that luxurious appeal associated with five-star hotels. It even had a rain showerhead. On a wooden ladder shelf sat various toiletries, white fluffy towels, and a few decorative vases. A single white oval vessel sink sat on top of a light gray countertop. I wanted very badly to hate everything, but I found myself loving it all and knew I would be very comfortable there. *Ugh!*

"I see Suzi has already redecorated."

"Uh, yeah. But the fixtures were my doing. She just repainted and put flowers all over the place."

She did more than that.

Kang's bedroom and office were on the second floor, as was another small bedroom that Suzi had taken over. "She uses it as a closet," Kang mentioned as we passed by.

"By the way, what time does she usually get back from the station, and does she know I'm staying here?"

"She knows, and she's staying at her mother's tonight. She thought it was best that she not be here since we would most likely be discussing the case."

"Oh?"

"You see? She can be thoughtful."

By the time I had finished my long, relaxing shower, it was ten thirty. Kang had already retired to his room. I guess we were both beat from not having any sleep the night before. I definitely had my eye on that pillow-top bed.

I checked Team Balkan's phone once more. Still no message from the mastermind. I started to think my plan wasn't faring so well. It might have been a long shot, but I had been hopeful.

I had just finished brushing my teeth when I heard a knock on my door.

"Abby, it's Kyle." His voice sounded hurried.

I opened the door and saw that he had jeans and a T-shirt on. "What's going on?"

"It's Ethel. I just got a call from her."

"Where is she? Is everything okay?"

"She's at a friend's house over in the East Bay, hiding. Not from us though, from Yee."

"Wait, why is she hiding from him?"

"Long story short, she got a strange call from him telling her to quit talking about him or else. She said his voice was low and menacing, nothing like the man she knew. That's what sent her running and why your agents were having trouble tracking her down."

"So he threatened her?"

"I'm not sure. She seemed frazzled over the call. She wants me to come get her. She doesn't trust anyone else. I'll bring her back here. I have a sleeper sofa."

"Nonsense. I'll take the sleeper sofa. She can have the guest room. Do you want me to come with you?"

"Nah, I'm just picking her up and coming straight back. It'll take forty minutes tops. I'll text you if anything changes, but it shouldn't."

"All right. I'll let Reilly know that we've located her."

Chapter 51

After Kang left, I locked the front door and walked over to the sofa. *Time to face my new foe.* I removed the fabric-lined pillows, and there staring back at me was the metal framing, cold and unforgiving. I pulled back on the strap and unfolded the creaking, wannabe bed. I had really been looking forward to a good night's sleep, but given that Ethel was older, it just didn't seem right for her to be sleeping out here. *Oh, the sacrifices I make.*

I sat on the edge of the bed and felt a bar push up against my thigh. *Suck it up, Abby.* To be honest, the mattress wasn't in bad shape, though I doubted the bed had entertained many overnight guests since Kang had purchased it. I stood and went in search of Kang's linen closet. I found it on the second floor between his bedroom and Suzi's gigantic closet.

There were a sheet and a comforter tucked away, but no pillows. I figured I would just grab one off the bed in the guest room. If I had to make do with a sofa bed, Ethel could live with three pillows instead of four.

I returned to the living room and threw the sheet over the bed like a fisherman's net, except my sheet didn't spiral out into a perfect circle. More like a crooked triangle. As I fitted the sheet around the corners of the bed, the proximity of my nose to the mattress allowed me to pick up a musty scent. Kang wasn't the type to use softener in his wash, so the sheet was devoid of anything that could counteract the noticeable odor.

I unfolded the blanket and fluffed up the pillow, hoping my nose would get used to it, but it just seemed that the smell had gotten stronger. Maybe I was the first to use the sleeper sofa and had unleashed years of pent-up stink.

When I finished, I debated if I should crawl into bed or wait up for Kang to return. I figured I had better wait, as I would probably be woken anyway when they returned.

I walked over to a small sitting area in a nook that was enclosed by three bay windows. It was located just opposite the narrow hall that led to the kitchen and washroom at the rear of his place.

I drew the drapes closed and shut off the main light, opting for the Tiffany lamp that sat on a table separating the two leather armchairs. A brass magazine stand stood at the base of the table. My options: *Cosmo*, *Self*, *Vogue*, *Entertainment Weekly*, and *Vanity Fair*. I grabbed the *EW* and settled in.

I had been engrossed with the new fall lineup of sitcoms when my nose twitched. I could still smell that damn bed. Or was it the magazine? I shoved my face between the pages and inhaled. *Nope, not the magazine.* I couldn't understand why the smell still lingered.

I turned my nose up and took another whiff. I certainly wasn't imagining it. I could smell it, but something about it bugged me. The more I sniffed, the more I realized it wasn't really a musty scent. And then it dawned on me. When my father broke out the good Irish whiskey, usually accompanied by his thigh-slapping rendition of "Rocky Road to Dublin," he would often light up a cigar. That was what I smelled, but why?

Before I had time to ponder my own question, my eyes caught sight of something in the dim hallway: a glowing cherry that grew bright, followed by a figure stepping out of the darkness through a puff of smoke.

Chapter 52

"Ethel?" I lowered the magazine into my lap. My eyes were focused, but I was clearly dumbfounded by who had just walked out of the dark and into the warm light of the lamp. I tilted my head slightly as I worked to make sense of things.

Ethel didn't have the broad smile I recalled seeing that first day we had met. Nor was she wearing a blouse with vibrant colors or an elaborate necklace draped over her chest. No, the Ethel standing in front of me was completely different.

Her eyes were concentrated and narrowed through her black-framed glasses. Her wardrobe consisted of a dark coat with equally dark pants. She brought the cigar up to her mouth once again and gave it a few puffs. A cloud of gray masked her stone-like face. "Didn't your mother ever warn you that if you frown too much, your face would stick like that?"

"What are you doing here? I thought Kyle…" I could feel a dull pain emanating from my concentrated brow.

"You haven't figured it out yet, have you? Come on, Abby. Up until a few seconds ago, I thought you were pretty smart. Wait, I take that back. Up until you sent me that picture…"

I shook my head. "It can't be…"

"Is it staring to set in?"

I had made a grave mistake. I had never once considered that the mastermind could be a woman. In that instant, my confusion cleared, and a deep hatred rose from my gut and into my chest. She was the person who had put a hit on my family. My jaw tightened, and blood engorged every muscle in my body, readying them to explode into action. Right then, I wanted nothing more than to impart great physical pain on the woman who dared to threaten my family with death.

I pressed both hands on the arms of the chair, but before I could stand, Ethel raised her right arm and pointed a gun at me. It looked like a .38 special. I didn't care. I could probably take one or two hits if she missed vital organs, but if she pulled the trigger enough, she could bring me down. Twenty feet separated us. I figured I had a fifty-fifty chance of reaching her before she pulled the trigger three times. Still, I didn't care. I had to assume she had the experience to fire it. I had to take the threat seriously, even if she was a short, unassuming woman in her fifties with graying hair. She might even surprise me by having similar skills to Sei. Still, I didn't care.

She brought the cigar up to her mouth and clamped down on the nub, holding it there, chewing it slowly. Her double chin jiggled as she puffed and chewed. Her eyes squinted even more as the developing cloud of smoke thickened. "I know you find it hard to believe that I'm behind the game," she grunted. "Most people do. Usually when they're dying, they come to grips with reality, but at that point, it's too late."

"What about Yee, the Triads, Jing Woo?"

She let out a short laugh. "Charles? I'm Charles, you idiot. Do you always lose your brain when you take your suit off?" Ethel shook her head disapprovingly. "For someone who spent years in Hong Kong, I expected you to have a better understanding of Triads. I don't blame you. There aren't many who do. Anonymity is how they retain their strength. It's why they'll never be defeated. Jing is easily replaceable, as are all members. It's a sacrifice each and every one of them is willing to make."

It took all I had to restrain myself. I wanted her dead, but I also wanted answers. "The Triads, women don't have a position of power within the organization," I said through gritted teeth.

"I'm not a Triad gang member. That's where you got it wrong, but Kyle"—she removed the cigar from her mouth, waving it to make her point—"he started to figure it out."

"You're talking about Vagabond Kung Fu?"

"I see he filled you in."

"He said it was folklore, overactive imaginations trumping up what is really just a band of two-bit thieves and killers."

Ethel let out a hearty belly laugh. "Oh, is that what we are? You can think whatever you like. Those who know too much never stick around to tell our story. Who we are, what we are: we don't care what others think. It's not important. Persevering, that's important. And the less people know, the more invisible we are."

Ethel squinted one eye as she looked down the barrel of the snub-nosed revolver. "I have your forehead in sight. It'll make a noise, but nothing too loud. Just a pop, but the force of the bullet will penetrate your skull easily, and I won't have to get my hands dirty."

"Kyle will—"

"Kyle won't. I have the poor boy's loyalty. I'm like a mother to him. He'll never assume. He'll never believe. And that's how I like it. How do you think I got into the house? He told me about the key he keeps under a potted plant out back. He's so trusting of me. No, Kyle needs to live. He's much more valuable to me that way. I need someone to unknowingly do my bidding within the SFPD. You, on the other hand…" Ethel lowered her voice. Her smirk disappeared, and her eyes seemed to darken. "You have no value. All you've given me is one big fucking headache. Chasing Chinatown was my baby. I spent years developing it, and now it's gone. Killing you won't bring it back, but it'll make me feel a little better. But that's not good enough. I want to feel a whole lot better." She puffed once more on the stalky cigar. "To do that, I need to kill your family. Slow and painful—that's what it'll take."

No, it won't. My heartbeat raced. My leg muscles tightened. My lungs drew a deep breath. Dying didn't matter to me at that point. I didn't care about myself; I cared about my family. I had to save them.

Chapter 53

Kang drove up and down the dimly lit street, looking for the address that Ethel had given him over the phone. It was located on Livingston Street, a largely industrial area dotted with warehouses, office buildings, and a few vacant lots near the Brooklyn Basin just off of the Nimitz Highway. He saw no one walking on the sidewalks, not even a bum pushing a shopping cart. He noticed a few empty cars parked on the street, but other than that, the area was deserted.

At first, Kang thought Ethel's friend might be one of those trendy artist types that lived in a converted warehouse space. He must have driven the length of the street half a dozen times before trying the adjacent streets, thinking she might have mixed up her directions due to the stress of the situation. But the more he drove, the more he became convinced he was in the totally wrong area. There just seemed to be no signs of any sort of residential building.

Kang was relatively familiar with Oakland, having made more than enough trips to the area's smaller and less popular Chinatown, but he still needed to punch the address into Google Maps on his smartphone. The pin squarely popped up on Livingston, so he knew it wasn't a glitch with the app. Ethel had specifically said, "1422 Livingston St. It's near the Nimitz Highway."

Kang parked his vehicle next to the curb and dialed Ethel's phone number. Straight to voicemail. He left a message that he was having trouble finding the place and that she needed to call him back.

His next call was to Kane. Her phone at least rang a few times before dropping him into voicemail. He left a message that he would be gone a little longer than they'd expected.

Kang sat quietly, waiting for Ethel to return his call. During that time, he thought about what she had said to him earlier, about how Yee had told her to keep quiet. Ethel hadn't been talking to the media. In fact, it was Kane who had pegged Yee as a person of interest. Kang figured Ethel probably told Yee that the FBI wanted to speak to him, but that hardly warranted the reaction she had painted over the phone. *Menacing tone, be quiet or else... Doesn't make sense unless he's hiding something.*

Kang tried Ethel's phone again and left a second message. *You'd think she would pick up the phone on the first ring the way she sounded earlier.* Without better directions, Kang was at a loss. *What to do. What to do...* He certainly didn't want to leave Ethel out to dry, but more importantly, he wanted to talk to her further about Yee.

Kang didn't know whether to be irritated or worried.

Ethel's actions lately had him somewhat confused; it wasn't like her not to return a call or to give a wrong address. In all his dealings with her, she had always been reliable and straightforward. The Ethel he had encountered over the last few days had appeared scatterbrained and unsure of her words.

Kang called Ethel once again and got the same response. He drummed the steering wheel with his fingers while he mulled the situation. He was out of ideas and had no other recourse. Plus, he didn't feel comfortable leaving Kane alone any longer than he already had. He should have picked up Ethel by then and been on his way back home. He threw his vehicle into drive and pulled away from the curb. *If I have to make another trip back to Oakland, so be it.*

Chapter 54

Ethel's tiny but plump body lay sprawled out on the hardwood floor. Her breathing had stopped after her fatal gasp, and her eyes remained open, even after the hard fall against the floor. The revolver she had gripped in her hand earlier lay a few inches from her grasp. A throw rug near her had begun to absorb the mess draining out of her.

Both of my hands were still white-knuckled from gripping the armchair. The burn in my chest prompted me to take a breath. I should have leaned back and let go a sigh of relief, but I didn't. I couldn't. Because standing in front of me and holding a sword that still dripped with Ethel's blood was my favorite assassin: Sei.

Apparently, any decision I had made up to that point, or lack thereof, had played absolutely no role in what had happened. There wasn't a scenario in my head that came remotely close to one that involved Sei killing Ethel. It had been the equivalent of facing an al-Qaeda operative only to have an ISIS operative kill him and take his place—same, same but different.

I didn't know what to think. I didn't know what to say. In my field of business, holding a conversation with a killer was a good way to prolong death, especially if said death happened to be mine. My weapon was still in the guest room, and I hadn't any idea how to get to it without Sei getting all Ginsu on me.

She stood still, knees bent slightly and the sword held out in front of her in a defensive position. Her gaze, cold and unwavering, pierced through me like a razor-sharp icicle. Slowly, step by step, she made her way around Ethel's body and toward me. I didn't know what to make of the situation. It seemed that each encounter I had with that woman left me with a plethora of unanswered questions.

"I'm a bit confused here," I eventually managed.

"What's to be confused about? I saved your life. A thank you is customary in these situations, don't you think?"

I wasn't about to entertain this woman's suggestion with an answer. As far as I was concerned, she was a cold-blooded killer. "Are you the mastermind, or is Ethel?"

"Those honors would go to her." Sei had stopped her gracious sidestepping toward me, though she hadn't lowered her sword, not even the tiniest bit. She might still have been assessing whether I was armed or not. I had no indication of why she was there. She certainly hadn't come here with Ethel, as the shock on the old woman's face when she saw the business end of a sword pop out of her chest had clearly indicated.

"I don't understand. Was she ninety days out on a

payment to you?" I asked.

"Always the jokester, aren't you?" In one fell swoop, Sei spun the blade around and expertly slipped it into the sheath strapped to her waist.

"Cocky move. How do you know I'm not armed?"

"You would have drawn your weapon on me by now. But seeing that you're dressed in shorts and a T-shirt, I highly doubt you're carrying a weapon."

"I'll go out on a limb here: You're not here to kill me."

Sei stared at me for a few seconds before answering. "Usually when people come into contact with me, it doesn't work out too well for them. You seem to be an anomaly."

"Am I supposed to be overjoyed? Grateful for your kindness?"

"A mouth like that will get you in a lot of trouble." Sei glanced around the living room. "Where's the detective?"

"She called," I said, motioning with my head to Ethel, "and asked him to pick her up."

"Doesn't take much to get you alone, now does it?"

"We thought the game might be over with Team Balkan's submission."

"The game is over but not because of your fake photo. You win, Agent Kane. You destroyed the game."

"And you killed the mastermind."

"It was either you or her," Sei motioned with one of her gloved hands.

"Why did you save me? And while I'm asking, I'd love

to know why you did so the first time. I know you were the one who dispatched Team Favela."

"You know so much, don't you?" Sei shifted her weight. "Not that I think I owe you an explanation, but since I'm in a giving mood…"

"Ah, philanthropist at heart."

"Team Favela was disqualified in Buenos Aires for reasons I am not privy to."

"How did he know I was the Attraction?" I asked as I shifted in the chair.

"His disqualification took place after the game changed."

"What? He thought killing me would reinstate him?"

Sei raised a shoulder. "I doubt he did any thinking, because his actions got him killed."

"Seems to me the mastermind wouldn't have cared who delivered my head."

Sei took a step back. "That would be a question for the mastermind. Whoops." She playfully pressed her fingers against her mouth. "Too late."

I leaned forward, readying myself to stand.

"Ah, ah, ah." Sei waved a disapproving finger at me. "Don't push your luck." She backed up toward the dark hall, obviously about to exit the same way she had come in. "As for an answer to your original question, I didn't come here to save your life, Abby. I came here to save the lives of your children. So long as Ethel was alive, your family would never have been safe. There are many like me who were loyal to her that could do the job."

"You mean you were given the contract for my family."

"Lin had the original contract, but when he failed, it was given to me."

"But you killed Lin, right?"

"Ethel bought the story you gave in the interview to the news station." Sei raised her left hand and flicked her thumbnail against her middle finger. "The head has been cut off the snake. You have nothing to worry about now."

It had become clear to me that, during this night, I had been facing a losing battle with Ethel and didn't even know it. If not for Sei, the nightmare I had injected my family and myself into would have continued. It never would have ended until she'd had her revenge.

I still wasn't sure why Sei had decided to spare my family, but I was grateful. Did she really have a moral conscience? Was there a bit of good under that hardened armor she wore? I suppose not every question in life has an answer.

"You said Ethel has many loyal followers. Won't word spread that you killed her?"

"Did I? Or did you?"

Sei stopped just short of entering the hall. Her eyes settled back on me once more. "Seems as though you misjudged me… again."

Chapter 55

By the time I had retrieved my handgun from the guest room and chased after Sei, she had disappeared—back to being a ghost.

I called House to let her know what had just taken place and to warn them about a possible attack.

"Everything is fine here, no disturbances, but I'll call in additional backup."

I knew my entire block had been on lockdown, and getting in and out would be no easy feat. Still, if there were more assassins like Sei, I had to believe that stopping them would be a serious challenge.

I had to hope that Sei had spoken the truth when she'd said the snake was dead. If she had indeed cut off the head, I imagined Ethel's loyal network of mercenaries would be effectively disbanded by that fact. There should be no reason to come after my family. We were still talking about contract killers; outside of loyalty, money was the primary motivator. If anything, they would go after Sei for killing the old witch.

I told House I would be over as soon as possible. I still had a dead body in the middle of Kang's living room, and I had yet to notify him of it. I gave him the heads up on a phone call but held back on the details, telling him to get home quickly.

CSI had just started to process the scene when he returned. I had already changed into jeans and a hoodie and had been waiting for him outside on the front steps.

"I can't believe it, Abby. I just can't believe it," he said as he exited his vehicle.

Kang was in serious denial. It actually caught me off guard. He had always been pretty even keeled when it came to work; nothing ever got him riled up or overly emotional. He had always been on point.

I continued to explain, but from the blank look on his face, the words that were coming out of my mouth were pole vaulting straight over his head. He would have to see Ethel's dead body firsthand to start processing the situation.

In we went.

Kang stood a few feet away from her. He kept quiet, mouth slightly ajar.

I moved closer to him, my arm brushing against his. "She meant a lot to you, didn't she?"

He inhaled deeply and let out a long breath. "I'm sad, I'm angry, but mostly, I'm confused."

"You're not the only one shaking your head at all of this."

"I feel betrayed." He looked at me. "She took advantage of our friendship. I enabled her to do a lot of harm."

"Hey, hey, take it easy. Don't go piling this mess on your shoulders. None of this is your fault. We were all fooled. And just to put things into perspective, it took one of Ethel's own to stop her."

Kang continued to shake his head and mumble about how he had never suspected, had never seen signs. I'm sure it had him questioning his own sanity. Ethel had been a trusted friend he had known for years who had often mothered him with encouragement. To suddenly discover that she was the psychotic mastermind behind the Chasing Chinatown game, well, that turned out to be one hell of a mind bender. Add that he had to also witness her bloody body in his living room—it was a combination of punches to the gut.

As much as I wanted to head straight home and see my family, I stuck it out with Kang until CSI had wrapped up their investigation. The kids and Po Po were asleep anyway. I figured I could catch up with them in the morning before I headed into the office. Reilly was expecting a thorough debriefing ASAP.

I fixed Kang a coffee and myself a cup of tea; fortunately, I'd had the forethought to bring my tin since all he had in his cupboards was the generic stuff. With both mugs in hand, I headed out front where he was seated on the steps. I sat next to him, pulling my knees in for warmth. The sky had just started to lighten, and soon the sun would be showing its face. The fog was barely a mist, as it had been most of the night. The last of the SFPD units had just pulled away, and Ethel's body was on its way to the city morgue.

"You know, there is a bright side to all of this."

"I know. It's over: the game, the killings, the bounty on your head. And I'm really happy about it. Don't think for one minute I'm not. I'm over Ethel."

"That was fast."

Kang pressed the coffee cup against his lips. I watched the point on his Adam's apple bob once. "She had innocent people killed for her enjoyment. I can't get around that. She deserved what she got. I have no remorse." Kang kept his eyes steered forward, probably churning over the events of the night.

For five minutes we both stared ahead, watching commuters drive by and little brown dogs on leashes relieve themselves. The first cable car rumbled down the street, its brass bell ringing as it came to a stop in the intersection. It was certainly a new day in the city. I relished the fact that the mastermind was dead, and so was her game. I was sure Kang did too. That investigation had tried our patience and tested our resolve to live. I was grateful that we had beaten it. A lot of people involved hadn't been so lucky.

I turned to Kang and gave him a playful jab to the arm. "Hey, what are you doing this Sunday?"

He took a deep breath and shrugged. "Not sure. Why?"

"Dim Sum Sunday."

"What?" His eyebrows crunched.

"It's my Sunday tradition with the family. We spend the day in Chinatown gorging ourselves on dim sum. Join us. It'll be fun."

Kang pushed his bottom lip up into a half-moon smile. "Why not? I'm all about dim sum."

"I'm really looking forward to getting my life back. I miss the routine. But hey, this time you catch your own perps."

Kang let out a vocal laugh. "You're never letting that go, are you?"

I turned my palms up. "I had a full stomach, two kids, and an aging mother-in-law in tow. The conditions weren't ideal, and yet somehow, I still managed to stop your guy. Not many people can claim that."

"Yeah, you're right. Maybe we'll see more of those moments in the future now that the Kang and Kane crime-fighting duo has been deemed a success."

"You mean Kane and Kang, right?"

"I'm not letting you have this one. It's Kang and Kane."

"E comes before G. So technically, Kane should come first."

"Yeah, but I'm taller."

"I'm prettier."

"I have a longer reach."

"I'm faster."

"Oh, you think?" Kang put his mug down, stood up and started to stretch. "Footrace, right now. First one to the end of the block and back has the final say."

I'm not one to resist a challenge. "This will be easy— and embarrassing for you." I put my mug down and started to stretch as well.

"The more you talk, the bigger the lump of pride will be for you to swallow."

"Just don't get all old on me and pull a hamstring, okay?"

We stood at the bottom of the steps. The intersection was roughly twenty-five yards away—fifty total to cover. Kang fished a quarter out of his jeans. "To be fair, I'll flip this in the air. When it hits the ground, that's the starting gun. Clear?"

I had both knees bent, my left leg slightly ahead of the other. "Stop yapping and flip the coin."

As soon as a few passersby cleared the sidewalk, Kang flicked his thumb, and the coin rocketed up toward a tree limb overhead, nearly hitting it. My eyes remained fixed on it as its trajectory upward turned into a descent downward. I leaned forward in anticipation, my heels lifting up and my breathing slowing. The spinning coin neared the sidewalk, and both of my legs were on the cusp of springing me forward.

Tink!

We shot out of our stances equally, but my tiny steps

propelled me into an early lead. I didn't dare let up. I knew Kang's long strides would eventually have him closing the gap. I concentrated on the corner and pumped my arms as fast as I could, calling on every muscle in my body to give its all. There was a lot of ego on the line.

As I closed in on the intersection, I began to weigh my course of strategy: slow early on and risk Kang passing me or take the chance for a hard stop. If I waited too long, stopping could pose a problem. Slow too early, and it would be akin to waving Kang to pass me.

I opted to slow early on, five steps from the edge of the corner. Even if that allowed Kang to catch up, he still had to slow down, and he had more mass to contend with. I knew I could again pull away quickly thanks to my small gait.

The scenario played out just as I had thought. Kang caught up, and we hit the corner's edge at the same time. Kang needed an extra step to stop and turn. I used that to my advantage. With my head down, I leaned forward and pumped my legs. My eyes closed briefly. When I opened them, I could see the finish line in sight. My peripheral vision told me Kang was still behind me. All I needed to do was hang on for a few more seconds, and I would have obtained bragging rights for life.

I closed in on the stairs, but so did Kang. I could hear his breathing and the pounding of his feet against the cemented sidewalk. A second later, he appeared next to me. I was slightly ahead, but he was gaining. I willed my legs to move faster. The burn in my thighs was excruciating. My breaths were deep and fast through my mouth. I gripped my fists tighter, my nails digging into my palms. My brow tightened into a vise-like cramp as I concentrated on moving my body as fast as humanly possible for a short woman. Tears formed at the corners of my eyes and streamed along the side of my face.

Kang had pulled up even with me. We seemed to be right in step with each other. We were almost there. Five steps. Four steps. Three steps. Two steps. Last step. Lean.

Chapter 56

The disagreement on who won carried on much longer than the few seconds it had taken us to race. Days to be exact—probably never an end in sight. Kang argued that he had me on the lean. I countered that I had thrust my right arm forward, and that gave me the photo finish. There would never be a clear winner.

With the investigation wrapping up, Kang would return to his duties with the SFPD and I to mine with the bureau. We had become friends, good friends, and I knew not working together didn't mean we wouldn't talk or see each other. We only lived five minutes apart.

To celebrate our fallen comrades, Reilly had organized a small memorial luncheon at the Cliff House near Ocean Beach. Reilly, House, Knox, Copeland, Kang, and I attended.

While gathered around a table overlooking the ocean, we raised shots of vodka in a toast to those who had given their lives in the line of duty. Agent Austin Tucker we lost when we were chasing Team Carson. In Bangkok, there was Detective Songwut Soppipat, or as he preferred to be called, Artie. Lastly, Agent Marty Castro, who CSI later determined had died at the hands of a traitor: Lin.

We talked about each one and shared our funny and touching personal stories. It was a nice way to remember them. Eventually, the conversation turned back to shoptalk as we each threw out our own theories on why Sei had killed the mastermind.

I kept my own theory to myself. I thought I had a pretty good one, too. I had asked Kang if he could return the teapot, hoping we could use it as leverage to entice Sei back for another visit since it was of value to her. I had left it on the night table near the bed before we'd left for his place.

Later when I returned to the tong to clear out my belongings, the teapot was gone. I asked Knox and Copeland if anybody had been up to the top floor, and they said no one had. In fact, they were the only people in the tong.

I checked the window. It was shut but unlocked. I could only assume that she had somehow gotten inside the room and taken her teapot. It was the only logical reason for it to go missing again. Though there *was* one more thing.

Before I left the room, I used the toilet. While I peed, I noticed a crumpled box in the trash bin. I didn't recall throwing anything away in the plastic bin, ever. Maybe Knox or Copeland had. Surely they could have been up here looking at the boards and had the need to use the bathroom, but I didn't think that was the case.

The packaging was a pregnancy test. I hadn't had sex

for quite some time, so I could safely rule out my need for one. Add that I was the only female agent on the premises, and it started to narrow down the owner. Only one other woman had access to that bathroom.

"I didn't come here to save your life, Abby. I came here to save the lives of your children."

Those had been Sei's exact words. Could that have been the reason for her change of heart? Had her motherly instincts kicked in? Was she retiring? Was that even possible for a person like her? I wasn't sure what to make of it. I used a pen to poke around in the bin but couldn't find the pee stick. *Of course she took it with her.* Whatever her reason for killing the mastermind, she had done me one hell of a favor. I'd like to think that not bringing up the pregnancy test with the group was my way of calling it even.

I looked at everyone gathered at the table that day, discussing the possibilities; none of it came remotely close to what I knew might actually be the reason. I couldn't help but think that I wasn't the only one who had misjudged her.

Chapter 57

The Cliff House sat perched on a headland overlooking the Pacific Ocean. While the others left quickly, House and I took our time. She had caught a ride with me. The sky remained cloudless, and the fog had disappeared, making for a stunning view from the restaurant. We couldn't help but snap a couple of photos of ourselves with the backdrop and enjoy the moment.

Eventually, I had the valet bring my car around, and we drove off. I always enjoyed House's company. Over the years we had become close friends. I had always had trouble making friends with other women; men seemed to be easier for me. But that wasn't the case with House. She understood me and didn't fault me for my ways.

We decided to take the long way back to the office, driving through Sutro Heights Park and then through the wooded Presidio Park. We eventually we found ourselves on Billionaire's Row, a stretch of three blocks along Broadway between Lyon and Divisadero Street. Elegant mansions with breathtaking views of the bay lined the street. They were home to people such as Larry Ellison, founder of Oracle; Ann and Gordon Getty; Congresswoman

Nancy Pelosi; and Mark Pincus, creator of Zynga and that addictive farm game.

House stared out her window. "The wealth that is concentrated in this one tiny block is ludicrous."

"Tell me about it," I mumbled.

"What is it?"

"What do you mean?" I asked, my voice stronger.

"You've had your eyes glued to that rearview mirror ever since we left the restaurant."

"Eh..."

"What?" House's tone signified her curiosity.

"I think there's a car following us."

House turned around and looked through the rear window. "I don't see anything."

We had just crested one of San Francisco's many steep hills. "Wait a second."

House craned her neck a bit more and waited. Shortly after, a forest green Mustang appeared on top of the hill.

Adaira Kilduff gripped the steering wheel tightly. Perspiration bubbled above her lip even though the air outside had been a cool sixty-five degrees and breezy. The tinted windows were rolled up to help keep their identities hidden. The air conditioner had been kept off. She preferred the warmth.

Alex, her butch-boi tagalong, sat in the passenger seat with a shotgun resting between her legs. Everything was phallic with her. On her round head sat large, on-ear headphones pumping bass into her ears. Her eyes were closed. Adaira couldn't tell whether she was asleep or not. It didn't matter so long as she wasn't running her mouth. Earlier she had kept making the same joke about how she was literally riding shotgun.

Putting up with Alex had grown old fast. Adaira hadn't thought it would take so long to get to Kane, but it had. She'd thought she could wrangle Alex into helping her kill the agent, collect the prize money, and disappear before she could adjust herself again, as if she packed manhood between her legs.

Adaira had known from the very beginning that a few days at the most were all she could take of the man-girl with bad breath, but she'd proceeded with her plan anyway, thinking it couldn't take that long to kill Kane. It had been well over a week. Patience had thinned.

Finding out the game was over didn't help matters. It only doused them with gasoline and tossed a lit match into it. *Having to put up with Alex's constant groping, her unintelligible musings, and returning oral duties on her unkempt snatch wouldn't be for naught,* Adaira thought. Someone had to pay.

Ever since the game had taken a winner-take-all aspect, Adaira had convinced herself that she could win. She believed it so much that at night, after what had become routine dyke sex with Alex, she would fall asleep dreaming of luxurious living far from her butch girlfriend. But as it stood, she had run out of money and was stuck with Alex's constant and incessant tongue flicking.

Earlier, she had parked off to the side of the road that led down toward the Cliff House restaurant, having followed Kane there. When the pack of agents exited the restaurant, her resolve to make Kane pay for putting her in that unfathomable situation had intensified. Seeing the petite agent in a joyful mood had only stoked her foulness.

"Alex!" she called out. "Wake up."

"Babe, I am up. I'm just chilling."

Adaira pressed down on the accelerator, prompting the metal monster to growl. "It's time."

"How long has it been behind us?" House asked.

"Since we left the restaurant, I think. Really, I only started to pay attention when we were driving through the Presidio."

"Well, there aren't too many ways out of the park. It doesn't seem out of place for it to be taking the same route. Make a left up here."

I turned onto Scott, heading north. A few seconds later, the Mustang rounded the corner. I took the next right at Vallejo. I kept my eyes glued to the rearview mirror, waiting to see if I had overreacted. Like clockwork, the Mustang appeared behind us.

"No way this is coincidence," I said.

"Pull over here." House pointed. "Let them drive by. Maybe we can get a look at the driver." The glare on the windshield had obstructed our view into the vehicle thus far.

I did as she said. We watched the vehicle approach, and just as it was about to pass us, it sped up, leaving us looking at a darkened rear window. "So much for seeing who's behind the wheel." I stayed put, and the Mustang made a left at the next intersection, which was convenient because I had planned to make a right so that we were heading south again, back toward the Civic Center.

"You're still jumpy from the investigation," House said. "It's understandable. You've been through a lot."

"Maybe you're right, but…"

"But you're wondering if this is another team."

"The thought had crossed my mind."

"Well, it's a pretty distinct-looking car. When we get back to the office, we can run a check on all newer-model Mustangs registered in the Bay Area. Maybe we can narrow it down. Forest green isn't exactly a popular color."

I dropped my car into gear and accelerated back into the street. I made a right at the next stop and tried to put the thought of the Mustang out of my head. I followed Pierce Street to Alta Plaza Park and made a left onto Jackson. I knew I could take that to Van Ness, and from there it would be an easy drive back to the Philip Burton Federal Building.

I had just crossed through the next intersection when I looked in the rearview mirror. The road behind us was empty. *Relax, Abby.* I shook my head and chuckled internally before looking once more. The Mustang was back.

Adaira punched the accelerator with her foot, and the back wheels chirped as they gripped the asphalt. The Mustang pulled into the oncoming lane. Alex pumped the shotgun handgrip once, chambering a round, before shoving the barrel of the rifle out the window. Her arms shook; it had been a while since she had fired a gun at someone. She licked her lips and lowered her head for a view down the barrel.

They were coming up fast on the Charger. Alex planned on unloading one shot right into the driver's-side window. Adaira had three GoPro cameras mounted inside the car to document the kill for the game; at least, that had been the plan when the game had still been active. Steve McQueen might have survived in *Bullitt*, but Abby Kane wouldn't. Even though the cameras were no longer needed, Adaira still wanted to capture it all on film—a personal memento.

They were seconds away from lining up with the Charger. "Now, Alex! Do it now!" Adaira shouted.

Alex pulled the trigger, and the recoil sent the barrel flying up, smacking the top of the window frame. She had missed.

"Shit! You told me you could shoot that thing."

"I can," Alex shouted back, "but she slammed on her brakes. Get me back alongside them. I'll get that bitch."

Adaira hit the brakes and threw the Mustang into reverse. The engine whined as the car raced backward toward Kane's vehicle. Alex pumped the handgrip once more and stuck the barrel back out the window. The Charger had begun to accelerate as well and was fast approaching but turned left onto another street before Adaira could reach it. She hit the brakes, shifted gears, and sent the rear wheels spinning as she chased after them.

The Charger turned right at the next stop, tires screeching. Adaira made the right with the same ease before hitting the accelerator again.

"Looks like they're heading toward Van Ness," Alex pointed. "We'll be able to pull up beside them if they do."

Adaira shifted into a lower gear and gave the Mustang more gas. They were right on the tail of the Charger. She tried to pull up along the driver's side but couldn't find a break in the oncoming traffic. Frustrated, she slammed into the rear of the Charger. It swerved a bit but quickly regained control.

The light was green, and the Charger didn't slow, giving Adaira the impression it was continuing straight through. But just as it was about to clear the intersection, the vehicle made a sharp left turn, the back end swinging out before straightening. Adaira hooked her steering wheel and followed suit. As they approached the Charger on the right, it quickly maneuvered over to the left lane, blocking them.

"Shit!" Adaira screamed in frustration.

"Pull up on the other side. I'll blast them from there." Alex leaned over Adaira and stuck the shotgun out the window.

The passenger-side window of the Charger lowered, and a handgun appeared and fired a shot.

Adaira hit the brakes and swerved behind the Charger. "They're firing back."

"You need to get me to the right side of the car. I'll cap her ass this time. I swear."

The Charger wove in and out of traffic, able to stay ahead of the Mustang, cutting it off every time it made a move to drive up alongside the Charger.

House grabbed the bucar radio I had installed and called the bureau's dispatcher. "Shots fired. I repeat, shots being fired. Vehicle is a forest-green Mustang with two females inside. Weapon appears to be a shotgun, possibly tactical."

"Are you currently in pursuit?" the dispatcher asked.

"Negative. The vehicle is in pursuit of us. We're heading east toward Van Ness."

"Roger that. I'll have all agents in the vicinity respond and notify SFPD to assist."

We needed to figure out a way to quickly contain these

two nuts. It was only a matter of time before they shot an innocent person—or us. We had no idea what kind of other weaponry the occupants of the vehicle were equipped with outside of the shotgun they had used. We couldn't take the chance of stopping to engage. We weren't wearing bulletproof vests and only had our department-issued Glocks on us. Even though I had a tactical shotgun in the trunk, the situation was too unpredictable. I thought briefly of ramming their vehicle but decided the better plan was to lead them to a less trafficked area while we waited for backup.

I turned left at the next intersection, heading west back toward Ocean Beach.

"Where are we going?" House asked.

"Back to Presidio Park. There's less traffic there and less of a chance they'll shoot someone. Hopefully, by then we'll have backup."

House remained in contact with the bureau's dispatcher, radioing our position. I pressed down on the accelerator, and the Charger shot forward, its wheels leaving the asphalt briefly as a small hill launched us into the air.

No sooner had we hit the ground than we accelerated up a steeper hill like a coaster making its climb to the top. The only difference was that we were doing 65 MPH, essentially rocketing forward on a ramp for all intents and purposes. I was familiar with the street and knew the hill didn't peak like others and immediately turn into a descent. It flattened at the top.

The Mustang inched up closer behind us, the barrel of the shotgun sticking out of the passenger window. I pressed harder on the accelerator, and the Charger exploded off the road at the top of the hill, clearing at least a foot and a half and remaining airborne for what seemed like minutes. We hit the ground almost evenly on all four wheels, the front left side taking the initial brunt of the landing. The vehicle bounced and swerved toward the right. I quickly countered and corrected. I looked into the rearview mirror just as the Mustang touched down behind us.

Ahead of us, a Toyota Prius had just started to enter the intersection of a four-way stop. I leaned on my horn, hoping to grab the driver's attention. I had but not quickly enough. I was forced to turn sharply to the left, the wheels gripping and screeching as we swerved around the Prius, narrowly missing it. The Mustang wasn't so lucky. It clipped the front end of the Prius, taking its bumper with it. But the Mustang hadn't slowed down one bit.

The flat hilltop would come to an end soon. The road ahead looked like the edge of a cliff. I was blind as to whether there was another car in front of us. I let off the accelerator a tiny bit but quickly realized that I'd allowed the Mustang to creep up along my side.

Bam! The shotgun blast caught the rear side panel of the Charger. A few of the pellets had caught the rear window. House didn't have a shot from the passenger side without sticking her body out the window and shooting over the roof of the car. That would have left her completely vulnerable to a shotgun blast to the face. Not ideal.

I gripped the steering wheel tighter. I had no option but to press ahead. "Hang on!" I shouted.

Five seconds later, we were airborne, soaring over the downward slope of the hill as if it were a ski jump. Nearly a quarter of the way down the hill, we touched down, front wheels first, followed by the front of the chassis. The jarring landing forced my grip to break from the steering wheel for a few seconds.

The Mustang slammed into the road with the same amount of force, bouncing up and down as the wheels struggled to retain traction. From there on, it was a straight shot back into the Presidio. The road ahead was clear of traffic, and I accelerated.

Into the wooded park we went, driving on a narrow two-lane. I had to lower our speed on the winding road, but still our tires hugged the turns loudly. Not long after, we heard the first of SFPD's sirens. Two units had come up behind the Mustang with blue and red lights flashing.

"Should we try to slow, sandwich them?" I shouted to House.

"We could try." House got back on the radio and worked with the dispatcher to coordinate with SFPD. One of the patrol cars sped up alongside the Mustang in an effort to block it in so we could execute a controlled stop. But no sooner had it gotten in position than the shotgun was turned on the patrol car, and two shots were fired, sending it swerving away, jumping the curb into the brush.

We needed a better plan. We would be exiting the secluded park soon and be back in the quiet streets of a residential area. That was the last place I wanted to lead our high-speed chase.

SFPD had radioed that a corridor had been cleared on Geary Boulevard. If we could steer ourselves there, they had more vehicles waiting and could try another controlled stop. Geary was a straight, four-lane highway. The conditions wouldn't get any better than that. A roadblock was out of the question, I told them. Whoever was behind the wheel was on a kamikaze mission.

We exited the Presidio and got onto Highway 1. The road had been cleared, and more SFPD units and as well as a few bureau cars joined the chase. I turned right onto Geary, leading the Mustang. From behind, a patrol car passed the Mustang until it drove even with us. Together we could seal off both lanes and start to slow down. But that didn't work. The Mustang accelerated and approached the rear of the patrol car and executed a perfect PIT maneuver, steering into the left rear corner of the vehicle and sending it spinning into the oncoming lane. No one had seen that coming.

More fire from the shotgun had me pressing harder on

the accelerator. The throaty growl of the engine rumbled up through my seat. SFPD tried once more to box the car and even tried a PIT maneuver themselves, but both times, the Mustang avoided the trap with the help of numerous shotgun blasts.

The Mustang moved up behind us and tapped our rear. If I had slowed just a bit, that tap would have turned into something much more. Geary had turned back into a two-lane highway, and we were fast approaching the cliffs that overlooked the Pacific Ocean. We had looped completely back around toward the Cliff House restaurant. A single metal guardrail to the right of us was all that separated us from the edge and a hundred-foot drop to the rocky remains of the Sutro Baths below.

The Mustang approached us once again.

"Abby, watch out!" House shouted. "They could bump us right over the cliff."

I'd had the same thought. It would be deadly if we were sent into an uncontrollable spin.

A loud *thunk* sounded as the Mustang rammed us from behind. I remained in control, swerving once. Up ahead, the road veered to the right. I knew I couldn't hug that curve with the speed I had the Charger traveling at.

"He's planning on running us straight off the road!" I screamed at House.

"Not if I can help it." House unbuckled her seatbelt.

"What are you doing?"

"Ending this!" House stuck herself out the window, her waistline resting on the window frame. She held her Glock with both hands and fired. The Mustang swerved behind us, crossing the lane before righting itself back behind us. House fired again, shattering the front window.

"The turn. I have to slow." I eased off the gas, but the Mustang maintained its speed. He was going to ram our vehicle right through the guardrail, even if it meant taking the plunge with us.

"Keep us steady!" House shouted. She fired twice more.

There was a loud popping noise followed by more screeching. The Mustang swerved from side to side. Each time, the driver overcorrected. The arcs widened. The Mustang fought to regain control. House had shot out the front right tire. It flapped around, sending chunks of rubber into the air and leaving only the rim. Sparks flew forth as the rim itself began to disintegrate.

I hooked the wheel to the left. *Come on, baby. Hold it. Hold it!* The car turned, the centrifugal force pulling my body to the right. House was still halfway out of the car and hanging on for dear life. I swear I felt the car lift a bit off the road.

My eyes shot to the rearview mirror. The Mustang couldn't hold the turn. I watched it slide across the road, the front right rim unable to provide any sort of traction. The vehicle slammed into the guardrail, uprooting a chunk of it

Ty Hutchinson 297

and taking it with it as it drove off the cliff.

I hit the brakes, and the Charger slid to a screeching stop. I turned back to see the Mustang in midair, soaring like a seagull heading out to sea.

It continued its arced trajectory downward toward the large, rocky formations that jutted upward through the crashing surf. It was on a path of collision with a towering mass of jagged rock that stuck out of the churn of whitewash like an exclamation point.

The front of the vehicle slammed into the hardened mass and crumpled like a metal accordion upon impact before the gas tank exploded, emitting a loud booming sound that reverberated inside my chest. A fiery ball shot up into the sky with thick, black, billowing smoke trailing behind it. The Mustang teetered on its front, almost vertical, before tilting to the side and tumbling off the rock and into the frothy waves.

The flames disappeared, and the column of black smoke turned gray and then white. House and I exited the car and ran to the edge of the road in time to see the bubbling ocean swallow the car whole.

Chapter 58

I couldn't prove beyond a doubt that the two women in the car were a team from the game, but when a recovery crew retrieved the car and bodies, there were telling signs. GoPro cameras were found. One actually survived the fiery crash, and we were able to review the footage. It had been attached to the driver's side. Most of the footage came from the POV from the driver's seat looking out except for a small snippet at the beginning. A redhead spoke into the camera and said, "I'm coming for you."

At the time, we were unable to identify the driver. The car wreck had removed most of her face, so we used a video grab from the camera to conduct a facial-recognition match. It came up empty. So did a search for a fingerprint match in our database. She was clean. No personal identification was found, though we were able to recover a smartphone. Unfortunately, saltwater had damaged it, making its contents irretrievable.

We were, however, able to identify the other woman. Her name was Alexis Cannon. We tracked down an address for her in the Castro neighborhood, where she worked part time at a small bookstore. Her employer had nothing good or terrible to say about her. Her coworkers said they hadn't known her that well, that she had kept to herself. The only information I had been able to pry from them was that they said Alexis, or Alex, had a new girlfriend. They didn't know any more than that. I suspect they had conveniently forgotten.

A week later, we received a tip from the manager of a hotel in the financial district. We had circulated information about the redhead along with a description and video grab of her face to all the hotels. We weren't sure if she was from out of town, but we took a chance.

The manager said he remembered seeing a guest fitting the description and had surveillance footage of her entering the lobby that we could review. The video wasn't the best quality and in black and white. We had to take his word that she had red hair. With that said, she certainly appeared to have the same body characteristics: tall, pale skin, similar length in hair. The passport information she had provided belonged to a deceased woman in the UK. Again, we were left without closure.

In my heart, I knew these women had been playing the game. My take was that Alex was a hired gun and the redhead was the actual player or at least the one spearheading things. I couldn't prove it, but at that point, it didn't really matter. What mattered was that the mastermind was dead, and the game had been shut down. So why had she still come after me? Had she not gotten the memo?

More importantly, were there others like her who would make an attempt?

I discussed that possibility at length with Reilly. "Abby, I think she was an anomaly. Maybe she didn't know the game was over, or she did but felt committed or something. There's no way to know." He shrugged.

I admit, I agreed with him on the reasoning. There was simply no reason for another team to come after me. It was risky with no monetary incentive. Then again, these people weren't exactly rational individuals.

I chucked the matter into a mental file. In all the years that I have served in law enforcement, I had put countless people behind bars and, in that process, made a lot of enemies. At any moment, one of my arrests could come back to haunt me. That was just the nature of my job and something I had to live with. I couldn't go on wondering if the next person I ran into on the street had a vendetta against me. I don't operate that way.

With the Chasing Chinatown case closed, it was time to get on with my life. And I had. I actually met a nice man, a financial manager. He wasn't Chinese, so Po Po didn't approve. His name was Greg and he was originally from the Midwest—Chicago to be exact. I had met him while the family and I were out enjoying Dim Sum Sunday. He had been eating in the same restaurant with a few friends of his.

I remember him walking straight over to our table, no hesitation, and boldly introducing himself to me. Right away he had checked off two items on my ever-evolving list of requirements. He was confident. I could have been married, considering I had children. Secondly, if he had come to the conclusion I was a single mother, it didn't deter him. I'm a package deal. No single servings.

While there seemed to be a heartbeat in my love life, I couldn't say the same for Kang. A month and a half later, he came to see Ryan compete in his first kung fu tournament. It was small, local, and mostly kids from his dojo and another. Still, I appreciated Kang's support. I knew it made Ryan happy to see him sitting in the bleachers with me. Kang had made good on his word and had two sparring sessions with Ryan. Twice that day, he was mistaken for Ryan's father. We had good chuckle over it.

"We make a pretty good fake couple, don't we?" Kang said.

"The perfect team."

"Yeah, maybe we should make one of those 'if we're not married by a certain date, we marry each other' pacts."

"Not a bad idea."

You'd think we'd be perfect for each other the way we get along and flirt. It's confusing. Anyway, about his love life…

"Suzi's moving out."

"Wait, what?"

"Having a corpse in our living room was the turning point. She was already on edge when she found out her driver had been murdered."

"I can't believe I'm saying this, but it seems like a natural response. Most people would have freaked out had they experienced the same."

"I think it's over."

"Didn't you guys just start dating again like six months ago?"

"Something like that. But my job, it's affecting her more than ever and not in a you're-working-too-late kind of way."

I threw my arm around my friend and gave him a hug. "Cheer up. You still have me," I said, flashing my choppers at him. "Remember our pact?"

"So it's on." Kang slapped his palms against his thighs.

"Sure. Why not?" I laughed and flipped my hair off my neck.

"I'll have to compete with Timothy Green for your attention. He's about your height, so he might have an advantage."

"I like my men tall." I hadn't yet told Kang about Greg and the three wonderful dates I had been on. After hearing about Suzi, I decided then wasn't the right time. It seemed like it was never the right time for us.

Or maybe it was.

A Note From Ty Hutchinson

Thank you for reading COIT TOWER. If you're a fan of Abby Kane, spread the word to friends, family, book clubs, and reader groups online. You can also help get the word out by leaving a review. If you do leave one, send me an email with the link. Or if you just want to tell me something, email me anyway. I love hearing from readers. I can be reached at thutchinson@me.com.

Better yet, sign up for my Super Secret Newsletter and receive "First Look" content. Be in the know about my future releases and what I'm up to. There will even be opportunities to win free books and whatever else I can think of. Oh, and I promise not to spam you with unnecessary crap or share your email address. Sign up now at http://eepurl.com/zKJHz.

There's a lot of procedure in the FBI, and I don't always stay true to it. If I leave something out or change the way things are done, it's because I don't think it helps the story. A dear friend of the family is a retired FBI agent, and that person does a pretty good job of keeping me in check, both verbally and with eye rolls. But in the end, I write what

Coit Tower

makes the story better, and that's the way it is. After all, this is fiction.

Visit me at my blog or on my Facebook page.
TyHutchinson.com
facebook.com/tyhutchinson.author

The Novels of Ty Hutchinson

Sei Assassin Thrillers
Contract Snatch
Contract: Sicko

Abby Kane FBI Thrillers
Corktown
Tenderloin
Russian Hill (CC Trilogy #1)
Lumpini Park (CC Trilogy #2)
Coit Tower (CC Trilogy #3)

Darby Stansfield Thrillers
Chop Suey
Stroganov
Loco Moco

Other Thrilling Reads
The Perfect Plan
The St. Petersburg Confessions

Printed in Great Britain
by Amazon